Minnesota
Mall
Mannequins

Here's what readers from around the country are saying about Johnathan Rand's *AMERICAN CHILLERS*:

"Your books are awesome! I have all the
AMERICAN CHILLERS and I keep them right
by my bed since I read them every week!
-*Tommy W, age 9, Michigan*

"I just finished THE MICHIGAN MEGA-MONSTERS!
It was the best book I've ever read!"
-*Stacey G., age 9, Florida*

"Johnathan Rand's books are my favorite.
They're really creepy and scary!"
-*Jeremy J., age 9, Illinois*

"My whole class loves your books! I have two
of them and they are really, really cool."
-*Katie R., age 12, California*

"I never liked to read before, but now I read
all the time! The 'Chillers' series is great!"
-*Lauren B., age 10, Ohio*

"I love AMERICAN CHILLERS because they
are scary, but not too scary, because I don't want
to have nightmares."
-*Adrian P., age 11, Maine*

"I just finished Florida Fog Phantoms.
It is a freaky book! I really liked it."
-*Daniel R., Michigan*

"I read all of the books in the MICHIGAN CHILLERS series, and I just started the AMERICAN CHILLERS series. I really love these books!"
-Andrew K., age 13 Montana

"I have six CHILLERS books, and I have read them all three times! I hope I get more for my birthday. My sister loves them, too."
-Jaquann D., age 10, Illinois

"I just read KREEPY KLOWNS OF KALAMAZOO and it really freaked me out a lot. It was really cool!"
-Devin W., age 8, Texas

"THE MICHIGAN MEGA-MONSTERS was great! I hope you write lots more books!"
-Megan P., age 12, Kentucky

"All of my friends love your books! Will you write a book and put my name in it?"
-Michael L., age 10, Ohio

"These books are the best in the world!"
-Garrett M., age 9, Colorado

"We read your books every night. They are really scary and some of them are funny, too."
-Michael & Kristen K., Michigan

"I read THE MICHIGAN MEGA-MONSTERS in two days, and it was cool! When are you going to write one about Wisconsin?"
-John G., age 12, Wisconsin

Other books by Johnathan Rand:

Michigan Chillers:

American Chillers:

Freddie Fernortner, Fearless First Grader:

Adventure Club series:

For Teens:

PANDEMIA: A novel of the bird flu and the end of the world
(written with Christopher Knight)

American Chillers Double Thrillers:

Vampire Nation & Attack of the Monster Venus Melon

AMERICA'S #1 SERIES FOR MAXIMUM CHILLS!

#8: Minnesota Mall Mannequins

Johnathan Rand

An AudioCraft Publishing, Inc. book

This book is a work of fiction. Names, places, characters and incidents are used fictitiously, or are products of the author's very active imagination.

Book storage and warehouses provided by Chillermania!©
Indian River, Michigan

Warehouse security provided by:
Lily Munster and Scooby-Boo

American Chillers #8: Minnesota Mall Mannequins
ISBN 13-digit: 978-1-893699-46-5

Librarians/Media Specialists:
PCIP/MARC records available at www.americanchillers.com

Cover illustration by Dwayne Harris
Cover layout and design by Sue Harring

Dickinson Press Inc. Grand Rapids, MI USA Job # 38697 05/02/2011

Minnesota
Mall
Mannequins

VISIT CHILLERMANIA!

WORLD HEADQUARTERS FOR BOOKS BY JOHNATHAN RAND!

CHILLERMANIA!

***I-75 Exit 313
then south
1 mile!***

Visit the HOME for books by Johnathan Rand! Featuring books, hats, shirts, bookmarks and other cool stuff not available anywhere else in the world! Plus, watch the American Chillers website for news of special events and signings at **CHILLERMANIA!** with author Johnathan Rand! Located in northern lower Michigan, on I-75! Take exit 313 . . . then south 1 mile! For more info, call (231) 238-0338. And be afraid! Be veeeery afraaaaaaiiiid . . . .

Sometimes when I think about it, I can't believe what happened.   In fact, it seems like it was all a horrible nightmare — that it never really happened at all.   Like it was a dream.

Or, at the very least, an *awful* dream.

My name is Jessica Harrison, and I live in Bloomington, Minnesota.   Minnesota is in the northern midwestern part of the United States.   It's in a part of the country where we have lots of lakes, and four very different seasons: spring, summer, fall, and winter.   Bloomington is a pretty cool place to live. The best part about it is that it's in the same city as the hugest mall on the planet: The Mall of America.   In case you've never heard of it, this mall is *so* big that there is even an amusement park in it, and not one of those dinky ones with only a couple rides. *This one is 7 acres big!* There are also over five hundred stores and restaurants.

Pretty incredible, I know.

But what happened to me in this mall is even *more incredible* than that.

My mom and dad have always been pretty cool about me going places as long as there is a chaperone. You know—someone older to watch over you. I do have an older brother named Mark, and I always beg him to take me to the mall, but he just got his drivers license, so he goes there with all his friends and leaves me at home.

But I wish my brother and his friends would've been at the mall on the most terrifying night of my life!

It all started when one of my teachers, Mrs. Shoquist, planned a field trip to the Mall. School had just started and this was the first trip of the year. In one of my new classes, we're learning how to run a store. Our whole class was really excited, especially me and my best friend, Rachel Owens. We love clothes, and we decided that someday we would have our own clothing store . . . maybe even our *own* line of clothes.

Rachel is one of the most popular girls in school, but she isn't a snob or anything. She just loves clothes as much as I do. Her favorite outfit is jeans with really fancy shirts.

That's one of the reasons that we love to go to the mall, to look at the clothes. We couldn't wait for this field trip . . . especially since Rachel and I had a secret.

We had decided that when we got to the mall we would sneak off to see the new clothes. If we snuck away, we could cover all of the stores and be back just in time to catch the bus back to school. Mrs. Shoquist wouldn't even miss us.

It sounded simple.

It wasn't.

We weren't just going to get into trouble . . . we were about to discover a secret — a secret that would lead to the most shocking, horrible experience of our whole lives.

2

Our bus pulled up to the mall at noon. We all had to wear school name tags, just in case we got separated from the group . . . which is *exactly* what Rachel and I wanted to do. We thought that we knew our way around this mall, even though it is so gigantic. It's so huge that people come to the Mall of America on their vacation—that's just how fun it is.

But it wasn't going to be fun today. Not for Rachel and me, anyway.

When we got inside the mall, the first thing we got to do was have lunch in a food court. Yum! There are lots of great places to eat, and lots of different restaurants to choose from. And, it was always so busy there that we thought this would be the perfect place to sneak away.

We each got to pick the place where we would eat. I decided to have Chinese food and Rachel went for pizza. We ate quickly, then just acted like we were taking our trays back. We were about to make a clean getaway to go explore, but the biggest blabbermouth of the whole class — Riley Kline — yelled out that we were leaving without permission. We stopped dead in our tracks. With quick thinking we ducked down into two other chairs and acted like we were still eating.

We thought for sure that big mouth Riley had jinxed our plan. When Mrs. Shoquist looked at us, we smiled and shrugged our shoulders like we didn't know what Riley was talking about. Mrs. Shoquist nodded at us and frowned at Riley. Then, when she turned her head we stuck our tongues out at Riley. This made Riley so mad that she finally just looked away.

When the coast was clear, we slowly got up again and snuck to the tray return. When we got there we looked around, just to make sure that nobody saw us.

"Anybody watching?" I whispered to Rachel.

"Nope," she replied. *"I don't see anyone."*

We stood there for a minute, then we ran to the other side of a big fountain and ducked behind it. We took off our name tags and stuck them in our backpacks, so that nobody would know we weren't where we belonged.

We were in the clear! Operation "Sneak-Away" was a success—or so we *thought*.

Little did we know that somebody was looking. From the moment we got off the bus, we were all being watched.

Not only were we being watched . . . but as we walked toward our favorite store, we were being *followed!*

Just as we reached the front of the store a large, freaky-looking hand reached out in front of us to stop us.

I gasped.

Rachel gasped.

We both jumped. We were in trouble now, but it was just the beginning of our nightmare.

3

A man glared down at us, and when we saw his face, Rachel and I gasped again.

Something about this man was *really* creepy. He had frozen black eyes, and a nasty snarl on his face. He seemed to be taller than anyone I ever knew, and he had slicked-back, black hair that almost looked plastic.

"What do you think you're doing?" he snarled, in a voice that made my skin crawl.

"I . . . I . . . we . . . we . . . " Rachel stuttered. She was so scared she couldn't even speak.

"We're with a class field trip, sir," I said. I fumbled for my name tag in my backpack to show him, but I was so nervous I couldn't find it.

"Then why aren't you with your field trip?" he sneered.

"We are! Really!" I replied.

"I don't believe you!" he shot back. "You're coming with me!" Then he made us walk in front of him. Rachel and I just looked at each other. Now she was more mad than afraid. But this man wore a blue uniform and a badge, and he carried a walkie-talkie. Our parents would be *so* mad at us. Mrs. Shoquist, too. I was sure that it would be a long time before we got to go to the mall again, if ever.

But what we didn't know was that it would be a long, long time before we even got out of the mall.

It seemed like we had been walking forever when I realized he wasn't taking us back to the group at all. We headed down a long, dark hallway. Our footsteps echoed off the bare walls and ceiling.

When I asked the man where we were going, he just glared at me with a blank, strange look on his face.

"Rachel," I whispered quietly without turning my head. *"He . . . doesn't look real!"*

"No," Rachel replied. *"He doesn't. He looks like a robot or something."*

We turned the corner to another scary, empty hallway. I had never been in this part of the mall before and I didn't think that Rachel had, either. He unlocked a door and opened it up. Behind the door was a room about the size of my bedroom.

"Wait in here," he ordered us in that creepy voice of his.

Afraid to make him mad, we did what he said.

He slammed the door behind us. Wherever we were, it was *cold* . . . and so dark that I couldn't see my hand in front of my face. We stood there, petrified with fear, too scared to move.

Then we could hear the lock turn, and his loud footsteps walking away. I knew we were in a lot of trouble already . . . but things were about to get worse.

4

The first thing I did after I heard his footsteps fade away was to try and find a light switch. I would be a lot less frightened if I could see where we were!

I groped in the dark until I felt something cold and metal and smooth.

The doorknob! The light switch had to be here somewhere!

I placed the palms of my hands on the wall and swept them around. After a moment, my left hand touched a small nub on the wall.

Please, I thought, *please be a light switch.*

I flipped it on and bright light flooded all around ... and Rachel and I couldn't believe our eyes.

We were in a tiny, box-like room. No windows,

no doors, nothing. Not even a table or a chair.

"Jessica, what's going on?" asked Rachel.

"I don't know," I replied, shaking my head. "Maybe he thinks we stole something." Which seemed silly to me because I would never steal anything in my life. Neither would Rachel.

Then I started thinking about that strange man again.

"You know," I began, "there was something very odd about that guy. Did you notice? He almost looked fake, like he wasn't human. Like one of those store mannequins."

"A *what?*" asked Rachel.

"You know . . . those fake models that they put the clothes on. They look like plastic humans."

"Oh yeah," said Rachel.

It seemed like we were locked in that room forever. Finally, after what seemed like a long, long time, we heard noises. Rachel and I listened as we stared at the door in terror. In a way, we were glad someone was coming for us, because we had been alone for so long.

But I was certain that something was not right . . . and that's what scared both of us.

Now we could hear footsteps coming down the hall . . . the same shuffling sounds that the guard made when he walked. But as the footsteps drew nearer, it sounded like there was more than just one person.

Then we could hear talking. I could hear a woman's voice.

"Rachel!" I whispered. *"That sounds like Mrs. Luchien, the mall manager!"* She was the woman that had come to our class to talk about the mall with us kids. Maybe everything would be okay, now that she was here.

Boy, was I wrong.

They were getting closer. Their voices became clearer, and I could hear that freaky-looking security guard saying that he had told our teacher that we were in the room and we couldn't get out.

"Splendid," Mrs. Luchien said. "Soon we'll have all of them. That's just what we need. The more we have, the better!"

Rachel and I freaked. All along, we had *thought* that something was wrong.

Now, we *knew* it.

And we knew something else: we had to get out of there. We had to escape somehow.

I ran over to a big metal vent in the corner of the room and tried to pry the cover off, but it was no use. I started digging frantically in my backpack.

"What are you looking for?" asked Rachel.

"Something to pry that vent off with," I replied. "We have *got* to get out of here!"

Rachel started to dig in her backpack, too.

"I've got it!" she exclaimed, and she pulled out her name tag and ran over to the vent. The thick plastic of the tag was just the right size to wedge the vent from the wall just enough so that we could pull it off.

On the other side of the door, I could hear keys jingling.

"Hurry!" I hissed frantically. *"They're almost here!"*

Rachel snapped the vent cover off just as I could hear the jingling of keys being pushed into the lock. I grabbed my backpack and followed her through the vent.

There was another room on the other side of the one we were in! I had thought that what would be behind the vent would be, well, you know . . . a *vent.* I didn't think it would connect to another room.

I reached back through the vent opening, grabbed the cover, and pulled it back on . . . just as we heard the door open.

Whew! That had been a close one . . . but where were we *now?* The room we were in was like some huge storage room with lots of boxes and crates.

"Where are we?" Rachel wondered aloud, her voice just barely a whisper.

"I don't know," I replied quietly. *"But look! There's a window over there!"*

We both tip-toed to the window . . . but when we saw what was on the other side of the glass, we both gasped at the same time.

"Oh no!" I said.

It was now nighttime.

"Man, we *have* been here a long time," Rachel said.

Just then, in the other room, we heard shouting. It was Mrs. Luchien . . . and she wasn't happy that we'd escaped.

"Find them!" she shouted angrily. "I don't care what it takes! We *must* find them!"

"Jessica?" Rachel peeped.

"Yeah?" I replied.

"I think we're in a lot of trouble."

I would have answered, but I didn't need to. I *knew* we were in for it.

And when a door suddenly sprang open and light burst forth, I knew that the real trouble had started.

5

"We have got to find them now!" I heard Mrs. Luchien scream. "We *must* find them!"

Wow, I thought. *What did we do to make her so mad at us?*

Rachel and I ducked down behind some boxes, and we didn't make a sound or move a single muscle until we heard the door slam and the footsteps and voices moving away.

From where we were hidden we could see another window, and on the other side of the glass was another room. A faint glow illuminated boxes that were stamped "WIGS." There were *dozens* of boxes of wigs.

"I'll bet that's where the security guard got his hair,"

I whispered. Rachel giggled.

We waited for a moment, hunched down behind the boxes. We wanted to make sure those two creepy people were gone.

"I think the coast is clear," said Rachel.

We tiptoed to the door. Luckily, it wasn't locked. We hurried down the hallway as quietly as we could, on the lookout for Mrs. Luchien and the weirdo security guard dude. We passed lots of hallways and corridors.

"*Gosh, Jess,*" Rachel said quietly. "*I hope we don't get lost.*"

Finally, we could see the light from the main mall area ahead. We knew that we had to be really careful, just in case they were waiting for us at the end of the hall.

When we got to the end of the hallway we slowly peered around the corner.

The mall was completely empty!

"Something is really strange," said Rachel.

"Yeah," I agreed. "There should be night crews around, cleaning things up and stuff."

Then we noticed that we were right next to Macy's, which is a *huge* department store. The main entrance door was wide open. I thought that was weird. Weren't they supposed to lock up all the stores at night?

"I bet we can get outside through Macy's," I said.

Rachel's eyes lit up. "I *know* we can! My older sister used to work there, and they always left the emergency exits open from the inside. You can't get in from the outside, but we'll be able to get out. Follow me!"

We ducked down and ran as fast as we could into the open doors and behind the racks of clothes. We needed to hurry, but we also wanted to make sure that no one saw us.

Just then, Rachel stopped, and I bumped into her.

"What's wrong?" I asked.

"Did you see that?" she said.

"See what?" I replied.

Just then, Rachel ducked into a rack of clothing. She was completely hidden.

"Jess! Hide!"

I slipped into the same rack, and now I was right beside her. We were both hidden within dozens of shirts and slacks on hangers. The fabric smelled fresh and new.

Rachel reached out and made an opening in the clothing so we could see around the department store—and it was then that I saw what had scared Rachel.

And now it scared me, too.

Mannequins . . . the plastic figures that were used to display clothing . . . were coming to life all around the store!

6

This was too far-out for us to even imagine. The plastic mannequins in the store were coming to life right before our eyes!

But how could this be? I thought about those old scary movies that I sometimes watched on Saturday night and I felt like I was in one of them. All around the darkened department store, these freaky things were slowly putting down their purses or their briefcases, or taking off their hats, scarves and ties. Then they would stiffly climb down off of their pedestals.

The worst part of all this was that they all had the exact same creepiness as the security guard and Mrs. Luchien. Their eyes were dead-like, and their movements were stiff and lifeless. We could only watch in disbelief as they slowly moved into the store aisles.

We sat there for a few minutes, hidden among the clothing, silent, not moving a muscle. We tried to calm ourselves while we figured out what to do.

"What is going on here?" whispered Rachel.

"I don't know, but that's the scariest thing that I have ever seen," I replied.

"I wish Josh was here," I said.

Rachel nodded. "Me too."

Josh Balcomb is a friend of ours. He's really smart and he's a lot of fun to hang around. Up until a few days ago, he was in our class—but suddenly, he was gone. His parents had called the school and said that they were moving away. Rachel and I were really sad because we didn't even get to say goodbye.

"We have to get out of here," Rachel said. Together we slowly stood up and peeked out through the clothing, just to make sure that we weren't seeing things.

We weren't. We could still see mannequins coming to life, walking in slow, jerky movements.

"Look, Rachel!" I whispered as quietly as I could. *"They seem to be headed towards the main mall area . . . like they're looking for something!"*

34

"Yeah . . . probably us," Rachel replied. Her voice and hands were shaking. "But I don't want to be around to find out. Let's get out of here. We've got to find an exit!"

I turned to begin to find our way out of the clothes, but I froze. I dropped my backpack. I couldn't move or speak, I could only try to grab Rachel, so that she would turn around to see this horrible sight—a sight that was far scarier than any late night movie I had ever watched.

Three grisly mannequins were standing right in front of the rack of clothing, just staring at us! Their plastic features were waxy, and skin-like. Even their eyes seemed to be alive. They looked like mannequins, but they also looked sort of . . . *human*.

As Rachel turned around to look, their huge, fake looking hands started to grab and tear at the rack of clothes that we were hiding in . . . and I knew right then that there was no way we would be finding an exit. We were trapped . . . and there was no way out.

1

Suddenly, Rachel screamed so loudly that it caught the mannequins by surprise. They paused for just a moment, and that gave us enough time to jump out of the other side of the rack and run the other way.

We kept running and we didn't look back, cutting through the clothing racks, zigzagging wildly through the dark store, hoping that we could outrun the strange mannequins. I knew they were following us and they weren't far behind. There were other mannequins in the store, too, and while we fled, I kept an eye out so we could stay away from them.

Ahead of us, near the back of the store, was a door that led to a stairwell. If we could only make it there, we might have a chance. I still wasn't sure how we were going to get out of the mall, but right now I just wanted to get away from the creepy plastic things that were after us!

"The stairs!" I shouted to Rachel while we continued weaving around racks and boxes of clothing. I pointed while we ran. "If we can make it to that door, we might be able to find a place to hide!"

We sprang to the big metal door. I reached it first, and I pulled it open. Rachel stepped through, then I followed, pulling the door closed behind us. My heart was pounding a mile a minute, and I was out of breath.

The room was some kind of office, with several chairs, a desk, and a few scattered boxes. Some clothes were piled on top of boxes near a corner.

"Over there!" I gasped, pointing. "Hurry!"

We ducked down in the corner on the cement floor and listened. We could hear heavy, thudding footsteps on the other side of the steel door. Rachel and I were both so out of breath that we couldn't do much more than gasp for air, but we were as quiet as we could be. I knew that if they heard us, it would be over for us. I didn't know what was going on, but the look on the plastic faces of those mannequins told me that they definitely weren't happy with us.

Through the small glass panel on the right side of the door, we could see the hideous figures passing by. But on the other side of the desk was something that I hadn't seen when we first entered the small room.

A staircase.

On the other side of the desk, I could see steps going down. The stairwell was dark, lit only by the glowing red exit sign above the metal door at the bottom of the stairs.

There it was! Our escape!

"Rachel!" I hissed. *"There's our way out! There's an exit!"*

We stood up, tip-toed around the desk, and hurried down the stairs. With every step my sense of relief grew, and in a matter of seconds, we were at the exit door.

We had made it. We were going to be safe.

I pushed the waist-high bar to open up the door. The bar didn't budge.

"Oh no!" I gasped.

"What's wrong?!" Rachel asked.

"This door! It's . . . it's *locked!*"

Rachel grasped the bar. We both pushed, but it was no use. The door wouldn't open.

"We can't give up," I said. "Maybe this door is just locked by mistake. Let's go try the doors in the other stairwells."

"But that means we have to go back through the store!" Rachel protested. "Where those creepy mannequins are!"

"We have to go back through there sometime," I said. "I dropped my backpack by that rack of clothing we were hiding in."

"I did, too," Rachel replied. "But I still don't want to go back there."

I looked at her in the gloomy darkness. Her skin glowed a faint red in the dim light of the exit sign. "We don't have any other choice, Rachel," I said. "We'll have to sneak through and find another way out. If we stay here, there's nowhere for us to go. They might find us, and we'd have nowhere to run."

"Yeah, I guess you're right," Rachel replied.

We tip-toed back up the steps, around the deck and to the metal door, peering cautiously through the window.

"See anything?" Rachel asked.

My eyes scanned the darkened store.

"All clear," I whispered, and I slowly opened the heavy door just enough to slip through. *"Come on."*

I stepped through and Rachel followed. As we were slowly creeping along, I poked my head up carefully to make sure that we hadn't been spotted. I couldn't see anything but racks and racks of clothing.

But I could also see something else: the main aisle.

If we can make it there, I thought, *we might be able to make it to another exit stairwell.*

"*This way!*" I whispered, ducking around pants and slacks on hangers.

Suddenly, I froze. I stopped so abruptly that Rachel ran into me.

Right in front of us, standing by a large, circular rack of blue jeans, were two gruesome mannequins . . . and they were headed right toward us!

8

The two mannequins continued walking toward us. Their movements were stiff and jerky, like they were robots. And for all I knew, that's what they were: robots. They certainly weren't real people!

But I didn't think we'd been spotted yet. The mannequins were coming toward us, but it didn't appear that they were coming *at* us. But if we made one move, I was certain they would see us for sure.

"*Rachel,*" I said as quietly as I could. I tried not to move my lips much.

"*Yeah?*" she replied.

"*Don't move an inch. Don't even breathe.*"

"*You mean, pretend that we're mannequins?*"

"Yes!" I replied. "That's it! Pretend you're a mannequin!"

Would it work?

We'd know soon enough, because the mannequins were only a few feet away!

I don't think I have ever been so scared in my life. The two mannequins were only inches from us, and I knew that if I even moved my finger, we would be found out.

But other thoughts raced through my head. *How could mannequins come alive? How could they move around like they were doing right now?*

It was all too unbelievable.

I held my breath, and the mannequins walked right past us. Rachel and I stood posed and waited until the two creepy figures were out of sight.

Finally, when I was sure that the mannequins were gone, I let out my breath in a heaving gush, and so did Rachel.

"That was too close," Rachel said.

"*Too* close," I echoed.

But we had spoken too soon.

Suddenly, Rachel shrieked. I spun in time to see four huge plastic hands reaching for us from the rack of clothing!

We were being attacked! Mannequins had been hiding within a rack of clothing!

Rachel tried to run, but she ran into me and knocked me over. I fell to the floor in a heap, which was bad enough. Then Rachel landed right on top of me!

Instantly, the mannequins were upon us. They emerged from the rack of clothing, their plastic faces frozen in anger. One was a man, the other was a woman.

There was no time to get up and run. In the next moment, the mannequins had grabbed us with their strong, vice-like hands. We struggled to break free, but it was just no use.

They had us, this time.

Now, we wouldn't get away.

Now, there was no escape. We had been caught.

9

Rachel and I struggled to get away from the two mannequins that held us firmly in their grasp. Strong plastic hands gripped my arm, and I wrestled to get away.

All of a sudden there was another hand in my face! I reached up quickly to push it away. The hand brushed past my face, but it felt different. It felt soft, not at all like the hand of a plastic mannequin. It was a human hand.

Rachel!

Then there was a terrible shriek. At first I thought it was Rachel, but it was much too loud for a scream that she could make.

"Hah!" I heard Rachel shout. "How do you like that, you . . . you . . . you plastic thing, you!"

I was still struggling with the mannequin that had a tight hold on me, but I knew that somehow Rachel had done something to the mannequin that it didn't like at all.

"Twist its head around!!" she shrieked. *"Grab the mannequin's head and give it a twist!"*

I reached around and grasped the dummy's head with both of my hands. I twisted as hard as I could. There was a terrible, mechanical shriek, and the dummy released its hold on me. The creature —whatever it was—threw its hands to its head, fell to the floor, and rolled away in pain.

"We showed *them!*" Rachel said proudly.

"What on earth is going on here?!?!" I stammered, climbing to my feet. I scanned the dark store, searching for more mannequins. I didn't see any, but I knew that there had to be more around.

"I don't know and I don't care," Rachel replied defiantly. "We can figure that out later. Right now, the only thing I want to do is get out of here and call the police!"

We began walking cautiously through the murky store. I turned my head from side to side as we walked, expecting a mannequin to come darting out from the shadows at any moment. Again, I noticed how strange the mall looked with hardly any lights on. It was eerie and dark, and I couldn't help but to feel scared. I bet you would, too, if you were in our shoes.

We entered the men's department where all of the mannequins had left their pedestals and were already out of the area.

Suddenly, I saw a figure on a pedestal and I jumped.

"What?!" Rachel hissed. *"What is it?"*

I pointed to a figure in the darkness. It looked like a human form on a pedestal, but I couldn't tell for sure.

"Is it a mannequin?" Rachel whispered.

"I can't tell," I whispered back.

Suddenly, I knew what it was.

It was a mannequin, all right . . . but it was one of those weird looking gray ones that don't have any face or hair. The ones that look like someone put gray fabric right over a person and glued it on them. They were just standing around as frozen as ever, displaying clothes.

"They must not come to life because they don't look human enough," I said to Rachel.

I felt another tinge of relief. Maybe we were going to make it out of the mall, after all.

"Jessica! Look!" Rachel exclaimed, pointing to a large desk area. "A phone!"

We ran over to it and I picked up the telephone receiver—but there was no dial tone! All I could hear was a really weird, loud, buzz, like crackling static. It was so loud that I had to hang it up quickly before the mannequins heard it. I was afraid that the noise would let them know where we were.

"Whatever is going on here," I said to Rachel, "I don't think it's very good."

"I think you're right," she agreed. "But it's night time. Someone is bound to come looking for us."

Rachel was right. When our parents discovered that we'd been left at the mall, they would come to find us. They might even come with the police! I sure hoped so.

I looked around the men's department. Shadows crouched like cats. It sure looked different without any lights on and no one around.

Except —

"Rachel," I said quietly.

"Yeah Jess?" she replied.

"How many of those gray mannequins did we see a few minutes ago?"

"I don't know. Three or four, maybe. Why?"

"Because now it looks like there are more."

Rachel turned to see where I was looking.

"You're right!" she said in a trembling whisper. "But they're not moving!"

"Just because they're not moving now doesn't mean they won't be moving soon," I said. "Come on! Let's get out of sight!"

Once again we began ducking through racks of clothing, trying to keep out of sight. I didn't know if the gray mannequins would actually come to life or not, but I wasn't going to take any chances.

It was hard to move within the thick clothing, but at least we were out of sight. I stopped for a moment, hidden behind a thick wool sweater, and Rachel mumbled something.

"What?" I asked her quietly. "I didn't hear you."

"I didn't say anything," Rachel said from behind me.

"I just heard you," I insisted.

"It wasn't me," she said with a shrug.

"Well, I know I heard—"

Suddenly, I stopped speaking, and in the next moment I knew where the mumbling was coming from.

We hadn't noticed that the group of gray wool mannequins had been sneaking up on us, moving closer and closer to us with every second!

They had come to life and before we knew it, we were circled by flailing gray wool arms and bodies that were making strange muffling sounds. In seconds, they had our clothes rack surrounded. They were pulling and pushing at us from every angle, and there were so many of them that I knew that we didn't stand a chance against them.

We were cornered . . . and suddenly the gray mannequins attacked!

This was it. We had managed to stay alive this long, but now we didn't stand a chance. The fuzzy gray mannequins were moving in closer and closer, and Rachel and I retreated into the thick curtain of dark clothing. The mannequins looked like big wool mummies. Their heads swayed back and forth and their long arms were outstretched, waving, searching for us, inching closer and closer and closer—

Wait a minute! That's it! They can't see because they don't have any eyes! They can probably hear us, and they only know where we are by the sounds we're making!

"*Rachel! Freeze!*" I whispered.

We stopped struggling and didn't move. It was really hard, too, because we were both so scared. The strange gray creatures continued to move closer, but now they seemed confused, like they weren't sure where we were. One of the faceless creatures reached his hand out, and I had to duck silently to avoid him touching my head—

But it was working! The gray mannequins couldn't see where we were!

If we were really, really super careful, we might be able to slip out right between their legs!

I looked over at Rachel, and she looked at me. I raised my eyebrows and mouthed the words *'follow me'*. Rachel nodded.

Slowly . . . ever so slowly . . . I sank to the floor. There was clothing all around, and I had to be careful not to touch the fuzzy gray legs of the mannequins. Rachel did the same, sinking to her knees and then to the floor.

Through the clothing, I saw a space that I thought would be wide enough to slip through undetected. I pushed a pair of pants out of my way and crawled forward on my hands and knees.

Closer . . . closer . . . .

I sneaked through the space, being careful not to bump into the many legs that were all around, then I chanced a quick glance over my shoulder. Rachel was right behind me, crawling on the floor. The wool mannequins were still standing around the circular clothes rack, mumbling and waving their arms. If I hadn't been so scared, I would have thought they looked pretty funny. I crawled for a few more yards before getting to my feet. Rachel was still right behind me, and she stood up, too. I placed a single finger to my lips and looked at her, indicating to her to remain silent. She nodded, her eyes wide and anxious.

We tip-toed silently away. We didn't exactly know where we were going, but I wanted to put as much distance between the gray mannequins and us before they found out that we were gone.

We darted around a corner and found ourselves in the boys' department. It, too, was dark and creepy, but I could make out racks and shelves of clothing. It seemed like in every different part of the store, it got eerier and spookier. As much as we were running, the store seemed to be getting colder. Shadows seemed larger. The Mall of America is really a fun place with lots of bright colors, but I have never seen it look so frightening.

And just when I thought that I couldn't be any more afraid, I saw another movement out of the corner of my eye. I jumped, but it was too late. A smaller mannequin—a boy mannequin, I presumed, from here in the boys' department—suddenly reached out from a rack of clothing and grabbed me by the arm!

"Aaaaahhh!!!!" I screamed, trying to pull away from the tight grasp. Rachel screamed, too.

I gave a sharp tug and tried to pull away, but the mannequin's grasp was too strong. Without hesitating another moment, I swung my free arm up and brought it down on the dummy's wrist.

"Ouch!" I heard a boy shout, and the hand that held my arm released its death-grip. Suddenly, a shadowy figure emerged from the rack of clothing.

Rachel and I jumped back, and we started to run.

"No!" the voice pleaded. "Stop! I'm not one of them!"

The boy's voice stopped me cold. I couldn't be sure, but he sounded familiar. I turned, walking slowly back to the rack of clothing where the figure stood.

"It's me! Josh Balcomb!"

"Josh?!?!?" I exclaimed.

"Josh Balcomb?!?!" Rachel said.

"Yeah! It's me!" he replied.

"How did you—" I started to say, but he interrupted me.

"Do you remember how I just kind of vanished from school?" asked Josh. Rachel and I nodded our heads.

"Yeah," I said. "We didn't even get to say goodbye to you. No one knew that you were moving until the school got that phone call from your mom and dad."

Josh shook his head. "It wasn't my parents who made that call."

"Then who *did?*" I asked.

"It was *them!*" replied Josh.

"Who?" Rachel and I asked in unison.

"Them! Those . . . those *dummies!* The mannequins!"

"Say *what?!?!*" I exclaimed.

"Do you remember when that comet passed over the mall?" Josh replied.

Rachel and I nodded. Last week, a comet was spotted in the sky above Bloomington. It was in the newspapers and all over the news, because it was so big that it could've destroyed all of Minnesota. It made the news because, unlike most comets, this one didn't seem to burn up, but rather, moved across the sky until it had passed by.

"Well, here's what I've found out so far. On the top of the mall there's a big antenna. That comet sent some sort of electrical charge to that antenna and into the mall! Somehow, that electrical charge did something to the mannequins and made them come alive!"

Josh's eyes were wide, and he was trembling. What he was saying seemed impossible . . . but we had seen the mannequins come alive ourselves. They had even attacked us.

"But I don't understand," Rachel said meekly. "They're mannequins. They're just plastic dummies."

"Yeah, but I've found out that there's a lot more going on," said Josh. "But—"

Josh was interrupted by a noise behind us. It was the sound of shuffling of feet and strange mumbling.

"I'll tell you the rest later," Josh hissed, *"but for now we need to get out of this store!"*

We fled, but Rachel was lagging behind. She was getting tired. I didn't know how much farther I could run, either.

"Grab my hand!" Josh said, "and lets keep heading towards the front of the store!"

"The front of the store?!?!" Rachel exclaimed as she desperately tried to keep up. Josh stopped and grabbed both of our hands and started pulling us along.

"Yeah, the front of the store where we can get into the main part of the mall," he answered.

"But Josh, wouldn't it be safer to get to a stairwell?" I asked.

"Yeah," said Rachel. "Or to an exit door that opens to the outside?"

Josh shook his head. "This way for now," he said. "Over here."

The three of us went through two swinging doors that led to some kind of storage area. The room was big and cluttered, and there were lots of places to hide. There were large boxes stacked all around, and we ducked behind a towering pile.

"You two really don't know what is going on, do you?" Josh asked.

"Well I know that those freaky mannequins are after us," I said.

"That is just the beginning of it," Josh said, shaking his head. "If we don't stop them, our entire planet is going to come to an end!"

I laughed. "What are you talking about?" I asked, still chuckling.

But Josh didn't laugh, and even in the dark gloom I could tell by the look on his face that he wasn't kidding.

"I'm serious!" he whispered. *"My family never moved! My family was captured by these mannequins!"*

A chill swept through my body, and I saw Rachel shudder.

"You . . . you *are* serious!" Rachel said.

Josh nodded. "And that's just the beginning. I'm telling you . . . we have to stop these things!"

"But what, exactly, are they?" I asked. "How did they come to life? I mean . . . they're just made out of plastic!"

"They're—"

Josh was interrupted by the sound of the double doors opening, followed by the thudding of heavy footsteps. Then the footsteps stopped, and the lights came on!

We huddled close, the three of us scared out of our wits. There was only one person whose footsteps sounded like that: The security guard!

And he was coming toward us! I could hear his boots plodding the floor, louder and louder, closer and closer.

He was going to find us!

12

The security guard was only a few feet away. In the next few seconds, he would be close enough to see us huddled among the boxes.

Suddenly, Josh picked up a doorstop that was within his reach and threw it over the boxes to the other side of the room. It thudded against cardboard and then skittered to the floor.

The security guard stopped coming toward us and headed in the direction of the noise.

"All right, I know you're over there," he growled.

Josh's eyes grew wide. He placed his finger to his lips and glanced at us. Then he nodded his head and stood up. He shot a quick glance in the direction of the security guard, then waved for us to follow him.

Rachel and I stood up. I looked over my shoulder and caught a glimpse of the security guard, or mannequin, or whatever he was. He was looking the other way, peering around boxes. If we were going to get away, we were going to have to do it *fast,* and we were going to have to be *quiet.*

Josh was already moving, and Rachel and I followed on our tiptoes, slinking around boxes and sneaking through the dim room. My heart was pounding like a hammer, and I was sure that at any minute we would hear the security guard shouting.

In seconds, Josh was at the door. He opened it quietly and slipped through, followed by Rachel, then me. The door closed quietly behind us.

"We've got to move fast!" Josh hissed urgently. *"We've got to get out of sight, and then I can explain what's going on here! Come on!"*

Josh took off running, and we followed.

The mall was dark, and I was trying to figure out where we were.

"What floor are we on?" I asked as we fled down the huge mall corridor. We darted around small kiosks that were closed and stores that were closed, but I didn't know where we were.

"We're on the second level," Josh answered as we raced along. "Between Macy's and Nordstrom's in the West Market area."

"But where are we going?" Rachel huffed as we raced along.

"To the restroom!" Josh replied.

"Now?!?!" I exclaimed as we dashed around a large kiosk.

"Yes!" Josh replied. "At least there won't be any of those creepy mannequins in there! We need to find someplace where we can hide, at least until I tell you more about what's going on."

"But wouldn't it be better just to get out of the mall?" Rachel asked as we ran.

"Rachel, we can't get out," Josh said. "They won't let us. I'll explain it all when we find a place to hide."

We ran through the dark mall, heading north toward Nordstrom's, until Josh suddenly turned to the left when we reached a place called Market Square.

"This way!" he said, and the three of us sped down the dark corridor until we reached the restrooms. "Come on!" Josh said, pushing the door of the men's room open.

"We can't go in there!" Rachel said, stopping at the door.

"Why not?" Josh asked frantically.

"Because . . . because . . . well . . . it's the *men's* room, that's why!"

"This is no time to be bashful! Besides . . . no one is around! *Get in here!*"

I slipped past Rachel and she reluctantly followed. Josh closed the door behind us.

We were in complete darkness, but only for a moment until Josh turned on the lights.

"I feel funny about being in here," Rachel said.

"Relax," Josh said. "There's no one else around. Besides . . . we need somewhere safe where I can tell you what I've found out."

"Yeah, just what have you found out?" I asked.

Josh shook his head. "You're not going to believe it. In fact, I'm not sure if I believe it myself. But here goes."

And when Josh told us what he'd discovered, my face went white with fear, and I realized that our trouble hadn't even *started* yet.

But it was about to . . . and it began when the door of the restroom suddenly burst open!

All three of us screamed at the same time. The door sprang open so quickly that we jumped and sprang back, certain that the mannequins had discovered our hiding place.

But I was shocked to see the panicked face of none other than—

Riley Kline!

"Man, am I glad I found you guys!" she said.

"How did you get here?" I gasped. I think that was the most I'd ever said to Riley Kline in my life.

"Same way you did," she replied. "I rode the bus."

"No, no . . . what I mean is . . . how did you wind up stuck here in the mall?"

"I was in one of the stores today and I thought I saw one of the mannequins move," she answered. Her eyes were wide, and even in the faint light I could tell she was terrified. "I followed it to see what it was, but it chased me down a back hallway. All of a sudden there was a whole bunch of them looking for me! I had to hide behind boxes so they didn't find me."

"But how did you find us?" Josh asked.

"You guys ran right by me. I was hiding under a kiosk near Market Square. You know . . . the one that sells calendars?"

We nodded. We had gone around the small kiosk just before turning and running down the hall to the restrooms.

"I recognized your voices," Riley continued, "and I followed you here. Man . . . I'm glad you guys haven't been captured by those dummies. I thought I was the only human in the whole mall. What on earth is going on here?"

"As far as I can tell," Josh began, "those mannequins have come alive because they've been taken over by creatures from outer space."

"What?!?!?" Riley exclaimed.

Josh nodded. "It's true. You guys know that my dad works here at the mall, right?"

We all nodded. Josh's father has worked at the Mall of America for a long time.

"Well, last week, my mom, my sister and I came to the mall to go shopping. Dad was working, but he was supposed to be done soon. Then we were all going to go out to dinner and then see a movie. When we couldn't find my dad at his office, we went to look for him. That's when we were captured."

"What?!?!" I exclaimed. "You mean you were actually caught by those . . . those . . . *creatures?*"

Josh nodded. "They took us to a secret cavern beneath the mall."

Rachel's hand flew up and covered her mouth "How horrible!" she gasped.

"And that's not the worst part," Josh said.

"How can it be any worse than that?" Riley asked.

Josh took a deep breath and spoke again, and what he said was the most shocking thing I had ever heard to this very day.

14

"Everyone who works here has been kidnaped and taken below the mall," Josh said seriously. *"Everyone.* Hundreds of people."

Rachel and I gasped in horror.

"You're making this up," Riley sneered.

"No, I'm not!" Josh said.

"Let him finish!" Rachel scolded. She didn't like Riley Kline any more than I did. Riley's face twisted into a scowl and she didn't say anything.

"Everyone in the mall has been taken?" I asked.

Josh nodded. "Everyone," he replied with a nod.

It took a long time for Josh to explain what was going on. He said that the comet in the sky wasn't really a comet, but an alien spacecraft. Every time the spacecraft passed overhead, it was sending an electronic signal to a large antenna on top of the Mall of America. This antenna was connected to the alien power generator which was beneath the mall. The aliens were capturing humans and transferring their energy to make the mannequins come alive.

"But what is it that they want?" I asked. "Why are they doing this?"

"The aliens know that humans will resist them," Josh explained. "They know that humans are fairly smart. The only way they'll be able to take over the earth is by using a human's energy, combined with their own energy, and transferring it into the mannequins. Mannequins don't have brains, but the aliens are putting computer chips into all the dummies. By using the life force of the humans, the mannequins will come alive. And the aliens program the computer chip, so it's almost like they have a brain—"

"—that's controlled by the aliens!" Riley finished.

Josh nodded. "That's what I think. Another thing I found out is that the aliens have also sent an electrical charge that moves through the walls of the mall. They've been able to lock the doors, so no one can get in, and no one can get out."

"That's probably why the phone didn't work!" I exclaimed. "When I picked it up, I heard a really weird squeal."

"The lines were probably filled with electrical energy," Josh said.

"How did *you* find out all of this?" I asked.

"I was able to escape before they hooked me up to the energy transfer machine," Josh answered. "Then I hid behind some equipment and watched. It was horrible."

"So," Rachel said, "are the people they kidnaped . . . are they . . . are they . . . ."

She was really having a hard time speaking, but I knew what she was going to ask.

"Are those people . . . *dead?*" I said, finishing Rachel's question.

Josh shook his head. "No, they're not. So far, no one has really been hurt."

"What do the aliens look like?" Riley asked. "Are they like ten feet tall with big heads and gigantic eyes?"

"I don't know," Josh replied.

"But what about Mrs. Luchien?" I asked. "And the security guard?"

Again, Josh shook his head. "I don't know," he said. "But Mrs. Luchien is in on the whole thing. And so is the security guard. They kind of look like mannequins, but they also look like humans. I haven't figured that out yet. I think that they might just be aliens in disguise. But here's the worst part."

Josh paused and looked at each one of us. I could tell that this wasn't easy for him, especially since his mom, dad, and sister had been captured by the mannequins.

"Tonight, when the spaceship passes overhead, it will send down another blast of energy to the giant antenna on the top of the mall. That blast will give the aliens enough energy to make the rest of the mannequins in the mall come alive."

"Big deal," Riley said. "How many mannequins can there be in the mall? A couple hundred? There are more police in Bloomington than that."

Josh shook his head. "The aliens have been using the energy to make their own mannequins," he said. "They've been doing it below the mall for over a year."

I shuddered at the thought. We've been to the Mall of America many times over the past year, and the whole time, robotic mannequins have been beneath the building, plotting to take over the earth.

"So . . . just how many—"

"Hundreds," Josh interrupted. "There are hundreds of mannequins beneath the mall. And tonight, when that spaceship flies over and beams down that ray of energy, all of those mannequins will come to life. Those mannequins will make more mannequins, and soon—"

"There will be millions," I whispered in horror.

Josh nodded. "We have to stop them," he said. "We have to stop them before it's too late."

"But how?" I asked.

"I have a plan," Josh said. "It's risky, but it's our only shot. Here's what we need to do."

Just as Josh was about to explain, we heard a noise from outside the restroom. Riley opened the door a tiny bit and peered out. She shut the door quickly and turned to us.

"*There's three of them!*" she hissed frantically. "*Three of those . . . those dummies! They're coming!*"

We were trapped.

15

We could hear the shuffling of hurried feet, and we knew that we would be discovered. The mannequins must have heard us talking, and were coming to get us.

"*Quick!*" Josh hissed. "*The lights! Kill the lights!*"

Without another thought I reached over and flicked the switch. The light died, and we were immersed in darkness.

"*Over here!*" Josh whispered, and I began moving toward the sound of his voice. I bumped into Rachel and Riley, then I bumped into Josh.

"*Duck down! There's a sink right here, and a waste basket! Get as far under the sink as you can!*"

Was he nuts? There was no way all of us were going to be able to hide behind a wastebasket!

But on the other hand, we had no choice. There was nowhere else to hide.

I fell to my knees right behind Rachel. Riley was right behind me. We crawled under the sink, and I heard Josh push the wastebasket over. It scraped on the tile floor.

All the while, we could hear the plodding footsteps of the mannequins getting closer and closer. In seconds, they would be at the door.

"Okay," Josh whispered urgently. *"Nobody move a muscle. Don't even breathe."*

I heard Josh shuffle one last time, and then:
Silence.

It was so quiet you could have heard a fly burp. I'm not sure if flies can burp or not, but if they did, we would have heard it.

And suddenly, the restroom door swished open. The light clicked on, but thankfully, it wasn't very bright. The small room was gloomy, like evening when the sun has just set.

My heart was pounding like a velvet hammer in my chest. Rachel's was too . . . I could hear it. I swallowed hard and held my breath.

Noises. I could hear the shuffling of feet as one of the mannequins entered the room.

Rachel huddled closer. I could feel her trembling at my side. Riley was on the other side of her, and I'm sure she was just as frightened.

Then I could see feet. Plastic feet suddenly came into view, moving slowly, scraping along the tile floor.

And when the creature spoke, I almost screamed.

"I . . . know . . . you're . . . here," the mannequin said. His voice was mechanical and robotic. *"I know . . . you're . . . here,"* he repeated.

I bit into my fist to keep from screaming. I have never ever been so terrified in my entire life.

The dummy continued moving, coming closer and closer with every step. He was so close I could have reached out and bit his knee.

Beside me, Rachel let out a tiny whimper, and I nudged her a little. I was as scared as she was, but if that mannequin heard us, it would be all over.

It might be too late already, in fact.

The mannequin stopped at the sink, directly in front of us. He turned and paused, then turned around again.

Suddenly, he turned again . . . and began walking away! I heard the door open. The light clicked off.

"Not . . . here," I heard his robotic voice say. The door closed, and I let out a gasping sigh of relief.

We waited beneath the counter for a long time, too afraid to move. We wanted to make sure that the mannequins were gone.

Finally, I got up. The room was inky-black and I walked, arms outstretched, to the door. After a moment of fumbling around in the darkness I found it. I opened it up just a tiny bit and poked my head out. The hall was dark, but I could still see well enough. There were no signs of any mannequins.

I closed the door, and the room was pitch black again. My hands found the wall, and I searched for a moment until I found the light switch. Then I clicked it on and turned around.

Immediately, I knew that something was very, very wrong. Riley and Rachel were still sitting beneath the sink—

But Josh was gone!

16

"*Rachel!*" I whispered frantically. "*Riley! What happened to Josh?!?!*"

A look of horror swept over both of them. When they realized that Josh was gone, I thought they were going to faint. I was scared, too. I was afraid of what those mannequins might do.

But I also knew that without Josh, we were hopeless. Josh had a plan to stop the aliens . . . but he hadn't told us what it was yet. If he was gone—

Suddenly, we heard a thump coming from one of the restroom stalls. A pair of feet appeared, and the door of the stall swung open.

Josh!

I breathed a sigh of relief.

"Sorry to scare you like that," Josh said, "but I knew that there wasn't enough room for all four of us to hide beneath the sink, so I hid in the stall until he was gone."

Whew, I thought. I was sure glad that Josh hadn't been carted away by that mannequin!

"Maybe this isn't the best place to hide," Josh admitted. "If they come back, we have nowhere to run. Come on."

He opened the door, peered outside, and waved us toward him. "Come on!" he repeated. "The coast is clear!"

He stepped out into the dim hallway, and we followed.

"Where to?" I asked in a hoarse whisper.

"Let's get back to one of the department stores," Josh suggested. "They are big and there are a lot of places to hide. I can tell you about my plan along the way."

We tiptoed back up to Market Square and turned left, heading for Nordstrom's.

"Keep looking all around," Josh advised. "They could be anywhere."

As the four of us made our way through the dark mall, I was once again struck by how eerie everything looked. The Mall of America is always such a busy

82

place with people all over. Now it was dark and cold and lifeless. It was a spooky feeling.

Finally, we reached Nordstrom's Court. There were several kiosks around, and Josh ducked beneath a large cart. Rachel, Riley, and I followed. There was a piece of canvas hanging over the edge, and Josh reached up and pulled it down.

Once again, we were in total darkness, the four of us crouching beneath a small stand in the middle of the mall.

Quietly, Josh began to reveal his plan. I have to admit, as he explained it to us, tears formed in my eyes. I was scared, but I was sad.

Josh's plan, I was sure, would never work, and we were going to fail. There was no way we could stop the aliens or the mannequins . . . and, after the spaceship passed overhead later tonight, the aliens would have all the power they needed to take over the world.

17

"We have to take down the antenna."

When Josh spoke those words, the three of us let out a gasp at the same time.

"What do you mean 'take it down'?" Riley asked.

"I mean we have to snap it in half," Josh said. "We have to break it so it won't work. If the antenna is broken, the aliens won't be able to send that beam of electricity to their machine in the cavern."

"But Josh . . . that antenna is probably *huge!*" Rachel said.

"It is," Josh said, "that's why it won't be as difficult as you think. The antenna is supported by long guide wires that are fastened to the roof of the mall. We have to get to the top of the mall and disconnect all of the wires that help support it."

"But that alone won't make it come down," I said. "The antenna is stronger than that."

"That's where things get tricky," Josh said. "We'll have to climb up the tower a little ways. The antenna is built in sections, and each section is held together by bolts."

"How do *you* know all this?" Riley asked. She sounded like she didn't believe him.

"My dad has a radio operation in his basement and he can talk to people all around the world. He's built antennas around our house, and I've helped him a few times."

"Oh," Riley said.

"Anyway," Josh continued, "we have to loosen the bolts on one of the sections of the antenna. I don't think that alone will bring the tower down, but I think that when the spacecraft high above blasts that energy ray down, the power will be so strong—"

"—It will snap the antenna!" I said, finishing Josh's sentence.

"Exactly!" Josh whispered. "Then the energy won't be able to reach the alien generators beneath the mall!"

"I don't know," Riley said. "I don't think my mom or dad is going to want me goofing around with a big tower."

"I don't think your mom or dad would like their life energy stolen to be used to power a mannequin," I shot back.

"Josh's plan is as good as any," Rachel said. "Who's going to climb up the tower?"

"I'm afraid of heights," Riley whined. I rolled my eyes and looked at Rachel. She rolled her eyes, too.

"I will," Josh said bravely. "I don't think I'll have to climb too high. Besides, I've done it before with my dad. But we'll *all* have to work at dismantling the guide wires. That's going to be a tough job."

"How do we get to the roof?" I asked.

"We have to get up to the fourth level," Josh replied. "My dad has an office up there, and I know my way around. On the fourth level is a staircase that leads up to the roof."

"Let's get moving, then," I said. "If we don't hurry it up, we'll be battling thousands of mannequins."

Suddenly, we heard a loud whirring sound. It caught all of us by surprise. Riley jumped and bumped her head on the bottom of the cart.

"What's that?" Riley whispered.

Josh leaned over and pulled back the canvas so he could see.

"It sounds like the escalator," he said. "It sounds like the escalator is running."

All of a sudden, he let out a gasp. I crawled next to him to see what was wrong.

Immediately, my body was frozen in fear. The hair on my head stood up, and my skin crawled.

The escalators had indeed started running—but that wasn't what was so scary.

What was so scary was what was *on* the escalators.

Mannequins.

Not five.

Not ten.

Dozens. There were dozens of mannequins coming up the escalator . . . and I knew right then and there who they were looking for.

Us.

18

Josh let the canvas drop to the floor.

"Holy cow!" he whispered. *"I didn't think there would be so many so soon!"*

"Now what do we do?!?!" I asked.

"We don't do a thing," Josh said. *"There are too many of them. We'll just have to wait to see what they're up to."*

And so that's what we did. It was maddening, hiding beneath that cart while we heard the mannequins all around us. We heard the escalator shut off. Some of the dummies seemed to be speaking, but we couldn't tell what they were saying. Mostly, we just heard the shuffling of their plastic feet as they passed by. Some of them came real close to our hiding place, and a couple of times I thought they were going to find us.

But they didn't. After a while, the sounds stopped. Josh carefully lifted up the canvas and peered out from our hiding place beneath the cart.

"See any of them?" I asked.

Josh shook his head. "Not yet."

Several moments went by while Josh looked around.

"Okay," he said finally. "Let's make a break for it."

"For where?" Riley asked.

"Well, if we use the elevators, they'll probably hear them, and they'll come after us. I think the safest way to the fourth level is to go up the escalators."

"But they'll make noise, too," Riley complained.

"No, we won't *ride* the escalators," Josh said. "We'll walk up them."

"Let's *run* up them," I said. "The faster we make it to the top of the mall, the quicker we can get started on the tower."

Josh drew back the canvas and crawled out from beneath the cart. I was right behind him, followed by Riley and Rachel. I was sure that I was going to see hideous mannequins popping out from the shadows, but there weren't any.

"We're going to have to be careful," Josh said. "When we go up the escalators, we'll be in full view. There won't be anywhere to hide. Everybody ready?"

I nodded, and so did Rachel and Riley.

"Follow me," Josh said, and he turned. The four of us slipped around darkened kiosks, along large, glass storefronts, until we made it to the first flight of escalators. Josh paused only a moment to make sure that we were behind him, then he bolted up the escalator two steps at a time. We followed right behind him, springing up the metal steps. Thankfully, we were all wearing sneakers, so the rubber soles didn't make much noise.

In only a few seconds, we had made it to the third level. I turned and looked below, but it was so dark that I couldn't see anything. There's an amusement park and lots of other cool things to see at the Mall of America, but without any lights on, it was impossible to see anything.

"One more level," Josh whispered. He spun and began sprinting up the escalator. My hope began to grow.

Maybe this will work, I thought. *Maybe everything is going to turn out okay after all.*

I was right behind Josh, Rachel was right behind me, and Riley was right behind Rachel. We hardly made a sound as we bounded up the escalator.

I shot another quick glance behind me to make sure that Rachel and Riley were keeping up okay. I know that Rachel was getting tired, and Riley wasn't a good runner, anyway . . . but they seemed to be keeping up all right.

I hadn't had a chance to turn back around when I suddenly slammed right smack into Josh. The impact knocked him forward, but he caught himself before he fell. Rachel slammed into me, and then Riley smacked into her.

"What . . . wh . . . what . . . happened?" Rachel spluttered, catching herself before she fell.

In an instant, I knew.

Josh had almost reached the top of the escalator when he had stopped. There, at the top, were two male mannequins. Their faces looked pasty-white, and their arms were outstretched like mummies . . . *and they were coming right for us!*

"Get back down!" Josh shrieked, and the four of us spun at the same time and began running back down the escalator.

By the time we realized our mistake, it was too late . . . because at the bottom of the escalator were two more mannequins!

We were trapped on the escalator!

19

The four of us bumped into each other as we realized there was nowhere we could go. Below us, two mannequins had already started to walk up the halted escalator, while above, two more mannequins descended upon us.

"We're surrounded!" shouted Riley.

"Lean back!" Josh screamed at us. "Lean back against the railing as far as you can!"

Rachel, Riley and I leaned over as far as we could, holding onto the rubber railing. I had no idea what Josh was up to, but if he thought that we were going to jump, he was crazy! We couldn't see down into the amusement park, but I knew that the floor was somewhere three levels below us.

I turned and looked at Josh . . . and I couldn't believe what he did!

Without another word, he spun . . . and charged at the two mannequins that were coming down at us! He dove right at their legs!

The result was just what he wanted. The dummies, knocked off balance, fell forward. They clumsily tried to catch themselves on the railing, but it was already too late.

One of the mannequins sprawled out on the escalator right at my feet and I lifted my legs to keep from touching it. Then the dummy took a tumble, then somersaulted, head over heels. The other mannequin fell, too, and began tumbling down the escalator!

"Let's go!" Josh ordered, and Rachel, Riley, and I sprang up the escalator. In a few short bounds, we were on the fourth level.

Below us, the two dummies that Josh had tackled were tumbling out of control . . . and heading straight for the other two mannequins that were coming up the escalator!

Suddenly, there was the sound of clattering plastic and some heavy thuds. All four of the mannequins fell into a giant heap, and they all tumbled the rest of the way down the escalator.

"Good job!" I said to Josh, patting him on the back. "That was awesome!"

"Yeah," chimed Riley. "That was cool!"

"Like mannequin bowling!" Rachel said with a laugh.

"Let's keep moving," Josh said, his head snapping around. "There still are more mannequins around."

The fourth level of the Mall of America was just as dark as the first three levels. There were no lights anywhere, and Rachel and Riley and I bumped into each other as we tried to follow Josh through the murky darkness.

"This way," he said, turning down a corridor. Here, it was very, very dark, and Josh seemed to disappear.

"Wait up!" I said. "We can't see you!"

"Stay right there!" Josh ordered us. "I'll go find the stairs that lead to the roof!"

"I thought you said you knew your way around here!" Riley said.

"Yeah, but not in total darkness! Stay here a minute!"

The three of us did as Josh said, only we ducked down by a water fountain. We weren't completely out of sight, but we blended in with the shadows.

Hopefully, if any of those creepy mannequins came by, they wouldn't see us.

"I hope he knows what he's doing," Riley said.

"Josh knows what he's doing," Rachel replied. "He's our friend."

"I'm your friend," Riley said.

"Some friend," Rachel hissed. "You tried to snitch on us earlier today!"

"Did not!"

"Did too!"

"Knock it off, you guys!" I interjected. "This isn't a time to be arguing!"

We remained quiet for a few moments until we heard Josh's footsteps coming our way. The three of us crept out of the shadows.

"Did you find the stairs?" I asked.

Josh replied by grabbing my arm. He didn't speak. Then he grabbed Rachel's arm.

"Ow!" she said. "Knock it off, Josh! Let me go!"

But I quickly realized something: the grip around my arm was too strong and tight to be Josh. It felt like I had handcuffs around my wrists. The hand that grasped my arm was hard and cold, and I realized why Josh hadn't said anything.

It wasn't Josh, after all . . . but a mannequin

20

I screamed, and so did Rachel. Our voices echoed through the dark mall. I struggled to pull my hand away from the tight grasp, but the mannequin held on strong.

"*Let . . . me . . . go!*" Rachel screamed.

But it was no use. The mannequin was far too strong.

Then Riley got into the act. Although Riley has never really been a friend of ours, she leapt forward and grasped the mannequins arms and tried to break the dummy's grasp.

"His head!" Rachel suddenly blurted out, remembering what we had done in the department store. "Twist his head around!"

Riley tried to grasp her hands around the mannequin's head. Rachel and I tried with our free hands, but the mannequin was able to duck out of the way.

Suddenly, something grabbed my free hand. I turned my head and gasped.

Another mannequin had arrived . . . and I could hear more coming!

Riley still hadn't been caught, but she still struggled to help us.

"Riley!" I shouted. "Run! There are more mannequins coming!"

Riley spun and leapt back. It was hard to see her in the gloomy darkness, but I could tell that she was reluctant to leave. She knew that we couldn't get away.

But it was better to have Rachel and me caught than all three of us.

"Go find Josh!" I shrieked as the mannequins began dragging me off. Another mannequin had arrived and was now after Riley.

Without another thought, Riley turned and disappeared into the dark corridor. We heard her footsteps for a moment, then they faded off.

Meanwhile, Rachel and I weren't about to be captured without a fight. Mannequins held both of our arms, but I pushed and pulled and tried to wriggle out of their grasp. With every move I made, the mannequins gripped harder and harder. My wrists hurt from the tight, vice-like grips.

"It's no use!" Rachel gasped. "They're too strong!"

The mannequins dragged us to the escalator. Just as we reached it, there was a popping sound, and then the sound of a motor starting. The steps of the escalator began to move!

The mannequins pulled us onto the moving metal staircase and we began to descend to the third level. When we reached the floor, they escorted us off, turned, and pulled us onto another escalator. Again, we were going down, and when we reached the second level, we were again forced onto another escalator that took us to the first floor.

And I knew where they were taking us, too. Without a doubt, I knew where we were going.

To the secret cavern beneath the mall.

When we reached the first floor, the mannequins dragged us off the escalator and we began walking through the mall. There was a bit more light here on the first floor, and I could see a little better. It looked like we were walking along the part of the mall called South Avenue. I could see panels and panels of dark glass, fronts of stores that were closed. We walked around dark kiosks and a fountain.

Suddenly, we halted. I looked around without turning my head. Four mannequins held us firmly . . . two of them held each of Rachel's arms, and two held both of mine.

They made us turn.

"Rachel!" I whispered. *"Look where they are taking us!"*

Rachel didn't say anything for a moment, then she realized where we were headed.

"We're going into the LEGO Imagination Center!" she whispered.

The LEGO Imagination Center is really cool. There are things made out of LEGO's that you wouldn't believe. Cars and buildings that are huge! It's like an entire city made out of LEGO's.

"But why would they be taking us here?" she whispered.

"I don't know," I replied quietly.

But in the next instant, I had my answer.

The mannequins made us stop. One of them bent down, and found a small latch on the floor. He pulled it up.

A door opened!

There was a hidden door in the floor! Light burst forth, and I leaned over to see steps that wound down.

With a mannequin on either side of me, they forced me onto the first step. Rachel was right behind me as we descended down the stairs.

So this is it, I thought. *This must lead to the secret cavern beneath the mall that Josh talked about.*

A lump formed in my throat. *What were they going to do with us?* I wondered. *Were they going to take our life energy to make more mannequins come alive?*

But more importantly, I wondered how we were going to get away. The mannequins were gripping my arms so tightly that there was no way I could release myself from their grasp. If they loosened their grasp only for a moment, I would pull away and bolt back up the steps. I thought about trying to push them over, but they seemed too strong.

Down we went, farther and farther. The stairs seemed to go on forever.

Finally, I could see a place below us where the steps seemed to end. A large steel door was on the right.

At the bottom of the steps we stopped, and I shot a quick glance over my shoulder at Rachel. She looked petrified. All of the color had drained from her face, and her eyes were big and wide. I think she was as scared as I was.

One of the mannequins that was holding me reached out his plastic arm in a robot-like motion, grasped the door handle, and pulled. The big steel door chugged open, and then the two mannequins pushed me inside.

If I could have screamed, I would have. It felt like all of the air had been sucked out of my lungs. A chill rose and fell up and down my spine, and my knees went weak. I thought I was going to faint.

I heard the other two mannequins behind me push Rachel through the door. Instantly, she screamed.

Never in a million years would I have ever imagined the horrible sight that was before us.

21

The door we went through opened up to a *huge* cavern . . . bigger than any store in the Mall of America. In fact, the room was probably bigger than a sports stadium! High above I could see steel support beams crossing the ceiling. The floor was cement, but the walls looked like they were cut right out of stone.

In the center of the enormous cavern was a giant machine with blinking lights that made strange noises. A huge computer terminal was built into it, and there was a big screen like a television. On top of the contraption was what looked to be a Ferris wheel on its side. The entire machine, including the strange wheel on top, was as big as a small house!

And mannequins.

There were about a dozen of them sitting at workstations around the machines, looking into computer monitors, chatting with one another in some strange language.

But worst of all —

People.

Hundreds of them. They were lined together on the far side of the cavern, side by side, standing. Not a single one of them moved. Their eyes were open, but they gazed straight ahead with blank stares. I could see store employees, managers, security guards . . . they were all here, all taken captive by the mannequins.

Or were they aliens? I wondered. Josh had said that the aliens looked a lot like the mannequins.

I couldn't stop staring at the hundreds of people that had been taken prisoner. All of them were motionless, like they were frozen. And another thing: they all had strange wires coming from their hands. The wires — hundreds of them — went up into the air and ran along the ceiling, then down into one of the enormous machines.

That must be the machine that takes their life energy! I thought. That's what Josh meant when he said that there is a huge power generator down here! I'll bet that's the machine that is connected to the big antenna on the roof of the mall!

The mannequins that were holding onto my arms ushered me forward. I took a reluctant step. My knees were weak, and I felt wobbly. My heart clanged in my chest. My mind raced, trying to think of a way to escape . . . but no matter what idea I came up with, none seemed like they would work.

A feeling of hopelessness fell over me like a blanket . . . but when I realized what was going to happen to me, the feeling of despair was replaced with another wave of horror.

The mannequins were leading us over to the group of frozen humans! They were going to hook us up to those wires and steal our life energy!

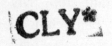

22

Again, I struggled to break free. I used all of the strength I could muster, but it was no use. The mannequins were just too strong.

"Jessica!" Rachel shrieked. "They're . . . they're going to hook us up to that . . . that *thing!*"

Other mannequins came over, and I was pushed next to a frozen human with a fast-food restaurant uniform. It was a woman. She was pretty, with long blonde hair tied back in a ponytail. But her eyes were blank, staring off into space. She, too, had those odd wires connected to her fingers.

Suddenly, the door to the stairs opened, and I saw a figure come inside. It was a small mannequin, and when I got a good look at it, another wave of terror about knocked me to my knees.

The mannequin was Riley Kline!

"Oh no!" I shrieked.

"Aaaahhh!" Rachel screamed when she saw Riley. I thought that she was going to pass out right there.

Riley Kline looked hideous. She no longer looked human. Her face was waxy and white. Her skin looked plastic. Her arms were outstretched, and her movements were jerky and mechanical.

Riley Kline had been turned into a mannequin!

The mannequins holding my wrists pulled my hands up. One of the mannequins . . . a man with plastic brown hair and a phony smile, held up a series of cables. At the end of the wires were small ringlets where they connected to fingers.

The dummy grasped my hand and held out the ringlet. Beside me, Rachel struggled to break away from her captors, but another mannequin came and grasped her hands.

As I watched, powerless to do anything, the dummy in front of me slipped the metal ringlet onto one of my fingers. Then he slipped another one on. Rachel, too, now was connected to the wires by the tiny metal rings around her fingers.

Suddenly, I began to feel very tired. I wanted to lie down, but my body felt stiff. It was hard to move my eyes, but when I tried to blink, they wouldn't close.

It was happening. Rachel and I had been captured by the mannequins, and now they were taking our life energy. We had tried to stop the aliens from taking over the world . . . but we had failed. I closed my eyes, knowing that it was all over.

23

I had just closed my eyes when a sudden, shrieking voice pierced the air. But it seemed faint, like in a dream.

Then I realized that I wasn't dreaming, that I was hooked up to that awful machine and it had started to take my life energy.

The voice jolted my consciousness. I was a little confused . . . until all of a sudden I was sent sprawling!

"Jessica!" a voice shouted. *"Rachel! Come on! Let's go!"*

Suddenly, the mannequins that were around us tumbled to the ground. Even Riley was on the ground, fumbling around.

But then a strange thing happened:

Riley jumped up!

"Jessica! It's me! I'm not a mannequin! It's just make-up!"

"What?!" I shouted.

"No time to explain now!" she answered. "Come on! Let's get out of here!"

Now I understood. Riley had arrived just as we were being hooked up to the machine. She threw herself into the group of mannequins, causing them to fall over. Plus, the tumbling dummies accidentally pulled the metal rings and wires from our fingers, so we were no longer connected to that awful life-draining machine.

Wow! Talk about luck!

I grabbed Rachel's hand and we bolted toward the door. The mannequins were already beginning to get back up, but they were slow and clumsy. I pushed one of them as I fled, and the dummy tumbled into two others and all three of them fell.

We reached the door and I stopped.

"Wait!" I cried. "What about the other people? We have to help them, too!"

Riley grabbed my hand. "We will!" she said. "But we have to get away or all three of us are goners!"

She had a point. We wouldn't be any good to anyone if we were captured. Right now, the best thing to do would be to get away from these creepy things, and make a plan.

And find Josh . . . if the mannequins hadn't already gotten to him!

Riley opened the door and the three of us wasted no time in making a quick exit. The door slammed closed behind us. I was thinking that there was no way we would be able to get away from so many dummies, but Riley had already thought of that.

At the bottom of the stairs was a folding chair. As soon as the door banged closed, Riley grabbed the chair, leaned it up against the door, and propped it under the doorknob . . . just as the mannequins reached it! The dummies tried to open the door, but the chair was propped against it and kept it from opening!

"Riley, you're a genius!" Rachel said. "I take back every nasty thing I've said about you in the past!"

"You said nasty things about me?!?!" Riley replied.

"Let's talk about it later!" I said. "Right now, we have to get out of here and find Josh!"

That said, the three of us sprinted up the stairs two at a time. Below us, I could hear the mannequins pounding at the door, trying to get it to open. For the time being, they were trapped, but I was sure that there must be another way to go into the giant cavern beneath the mall, and it would only be a matter of time before they came after us.

After a few moments, we reached the top of the stairs. All three of us were huffing and puffing, out of breath from the dash up the steps.

"To the fourth level!" I shouted. "We've got to find Josh and help him!"

We ran over to the nearest escalator. It wasn't operating, of course, and we had to run up the metal steps. Which wasn't easy, since we were all pretty tired already.

By the time we made it to the second level, my heart was pounding so hard I thought it was going to explode right out of my chest. When we reached the third level, I was taking huge, deep breaths, gasping for air. And by the time we reached the fourth level, we had to rest. We stopped at the top of the escalator. Rachel fell to her knees, gasping. We were exhausted.

"Well, there's one good thing," I said in between gasps.

"What?" Rachel huffed.

"We haven't seen any of those gross mannequins."

But when I saw two shadows coming out of a darkened corridor, I realized that I had spoken too soon.

24

"*Don't move!*" Rachel hissed.

The three of us froze where we were, kneeling on the floor at the top of the escalator. Our only hope was that the mannequins wouldn't see us. If they were going to use this escalator to go down to the third floor, we were in a lot of trouble.

But what was really difficult was trying to remain quiet. I was so out of breath that my lungs felt like they were on fire, yet I didn't dare take in the huge gulps of air that I so desperately wanted. Instead, I inhaled long and slow, and held my breath. Riley and Rachel did the same.

I could hear the mannequins moving, and I knew they were coming closer. In the darkness, it looked like there were only two of them. I was hopeful, because I figured that if there were only two of them, Rachel and Riley and I could probably fight them off.

There was one thing for sure: I wasn't going back down into that under-the-mall-prison!

The mannequins continued coming, and I began to realize that they were, in fact, heading in our direction, and they probably were going to go down to the next level using the escalator that we'd just ran up. It was very dark, but I was sure that they'd see us when they got closer.

I looked at Rachel, and she looked at me. I mouthed the word *'push'*, and Rachel understood, gently nodding her head. When the dummies got close enough, we would push them down the escalator.

Now we could see them clearly, and I could hear their plastic feet shuffling against the cold, smooth floor. Thankfully, they hadn't spotted us yet. I think that we just blended in with the other shadows.

But I knew that once the mannequins were close enough, they'd see us for sure, since the three of us were right in front of the escalator.

Moments later, the mannequins were only a few feet away.

"Now!" I shouted, springing to my feet. Rachel did the same, but Riley didn't. Instead, she crouched down on her hands and knees in front of the escalator.

Rachel and I darted around the mannequins so we were behind them. We caught them completely by surprise, and they didn't have time to react.

"*Go! Go! Go!*" Rachel shouted, and with that, we both gave the two dummies heaving shoves. They tumbled forward, out of balance, but when they hit Riley Kline, it was all over. The two mannequins fell over her and began bouncing down the escalator, out of control, flipping over and tumbling head over heels.

"*Let's go!*" I said, not wanting to wait and see if the mannequins would gather themselves together and come after us.

We headed in the direction that we thought Josh had gone. I was hoping we might be able to find that door he was talking about that led up to the roof.

But in the back of my mind, there was also something else that bothered me.

What if the mannequins had captured him? We hadn't seen him since he headed down the dark corridor to find the door . . . right before the mannequins captured us and took us below the mall. What if he had been captured, too? Then what?

Regardless, we didn't have a choice. We were going to have to destroy the antenna at the top of the mall with or without Josh.

But first we'd have to figure out how to get there.

"Man, I wish we had a light," Riley said. "It sure is dark."

We made our way along the black corridor, and I dragged my finger along the wall, just in case there was a light switch somewhere.

Up ahead we could see a faint glow. When we got closer, we discovered a large window. We stopped and stared out.

Far below us was the city. Beyond the perimeter of the mall, the city buzzed. Dots of light—cars and trucks—traveled along narrow roads, and the lights of the city lit up the sky. I wondered if anyone in Bloomington knew of the danger we were all in.

"Come on," I said, and I began walking again. "We've got to find Josh."

We tiptoed down the corridor. Along the way, we found several doors. I peeked into a few of them, but it looked like they were only offices.

Finally, after walking for a few minutes, we came to a door. It was a bigger door than most of the office doors, and it was made of steel. There wasn't a window we could see through, but I was certain that it had to be the door we were looking for.

"This has to be it!" Rachel whispered excitedly. She grasped a long metal bar on the door.

"Be careful," I said. "You don't know what might be on the other side."

Carefully, Rachel pushed. There was a click and a chug, and the door squeaked open. Rachel opened it just wide enough to poke her head through. Then she drew back.

"Stairs!" she exclaimed. *"There are stairs that go up to another door!"*

I peered around the open door.

Rachel was right!

Stairs led up to another metal door. On the ceiling, a single light bulb burned, but it didn't provide much light.

"Let's go check it out," Riley said, and she pushed the door open. The three of us stepped into the dimly lit stairway, and walked up the steps. In a few moments, we were at the top, standing on a small landing. In front of us was a door.

"This is it!" I said, pointing to a sign on the wall. A small, rectangular plate had the words *CAUTION: ROOFTOP* printed in bold letters.

Without another word, I grasped the bar and pushed. The door was heavy. It opened about an inch, and cool night air whispered against my face.

"Help me get this open," I said, and Rachel placed her hands on the bar. Riley put her hands on the door, and we pushed.

The door swung open, and the three of us screamed.

There were two shapes right in front of us — and there was no doubt who they were.

The security guard and Mrs. Luchien!

25

There had been so much going on that I had forgotten about them. Now, as we stood only a few feet away from them, I was filled with horror.

Because I knew what they were.

Aliens.

Not humans. Not mannequins.

Aliens. They had to be. Their skin was kind of shiny, like it was made out of plastic, and their eyes were like glass. They looked weird.

But then I noticed someone else:

Josh!

Just like he had said, there was an antenna here on the roof . . . and it was huge! It towered up into the night sky. Way up at the very top, a red light blinked.

The antenna was about fifty feet from where we stood . . . and Josh was climbing up it! I could see his dark shape silhouetted against the black, star-filled sky. He hadn't gone very far, yet . . . and I hoped he wasn't going to climb too high. Climbing a tower can be really dangerous.

The alien security guard took a step in our direction. There was a scowl on his face that told me right away that this time he meant *business.*

"*Run!*" I shouted, and I darted away from him. "*Split up! They can't catch all three of us!*"

We took off in three different directions, and the security guard stopped and snapped his head around as if he didn't know who to chase first.

The roof of the mall was flat. It appeared to be covered by a soft, rubber-like substance, and my sneakers gripped the surface tightly. Which was a good thing, because I sure didn't want to slip now!

There were several guide wires that I had to avoid. The wires were as thick as my thumb and shot up into the sky toward the tower. These were the ones that Josh had said helped support the antenna.

"*Leave them!*" I heard Mrs. Luchien scream to the security guard. "*Forget about them! We've got to stop him from damaging the antenna!*"

126

I turned around. Rachel and Riley were both safe distances from Mrs. Luchien and the security guard.

I looked up. On the antenna, Josh had stopped climbing and was holding something in his hand. It looked like it was some kind of tool or something, and as I watched, he began using it to unbolt or unscrew something on the large metal tower.

"Stop him!" Mrs. Luchien shrieked, and the security guard sprang. He ran across the roof to the base of the tower, grabbed hold of a metal rung, and began to climb.

"Josh!" I shouted. *"Watch out! He's coming up after you!"*

"I'll take care of him!" he shouted down to me. "You guys unbolt the guide wires!"

I turned to the guide wire that was closest to me. It was connected to the roof by a series of large bolts. I thought that there was no way I would be able to unscrew them without a wrench, but when I tried to turn it with my hand, it moved. It was difficult, but I managed.

I shot a quick glance across the dark roof. Rachel and Riley were doing the same thing I was doing. Mrs. Luchien stood by the door, screaming up at the security guard.

"Stop him!!" she was ordering. *"You must stop him now! The spacecraft will be overhead at any moment!"*

The alien security guard was climbing up the tower, but he wasn't moving very fast. He seemed awkward and slow. But I knew that it wouldn't be long before he reached Josh. I hoped that Josh would be able to complete his work loosening the bolts before the guard reached him.

"Hurry, Josh!" I heard Rachel shout up to him, and her voice echoed across the rooftop. While I turned the bolts that fastened the guide wires, I kept glancing up at Josh.

Suddenly, a movement caught my eye. It was a long ways away, high in the sky. It was bright, it was moving fast, and it was coming toward the mall. It was so high in the sky that it looked like a comet, like a little dot of white moving quickly.

But I knew that it wasn't a comet. It wasn't an airplane or a helicopter. In fact, it wasn't anything from this earth.

It was the spaceship—

And if it kept moving as fast as it was, it was going to be right over us in less than a minute!

26

"Josh!" I shrieked. *"The spacecraft! It's coming!"*

Josh paused only for a moment, glanced up quickly into the night sky, then returned to his work.

"Never mind me!" he shouted down to us. "Just make sure you loosen those cables! Hurry!"

I had finally finished unfastening the bolts on the cable I had been working on, and I dashed several feet over to another one. Rachel was working on another one, too, and then I saw Riley run to another cable and get to work. And high in the sky, the spacecraft kept coming, flying faster than I had ever seen anything move in my life. It was a race against the clock. We had to get the cables loose before the alien spacecraft had a chance to shoot down its ray of energy.

I heard a shout from above and I turned my head. The security guard was now only a few feet from Josh . . . and Josh was now climbing higher to get away from him! The security guard reached up and tried to grab Josh's foot, but Josh was able to pull it away just in time.

Problem was, Josh still had to get down before the spaceship passed overhead. I didn't know what would happen if the spacecraft shot its beam down while Josh was still on the antenna, but I knew that it wouldn't be good.

"Josh!" I shouted. "You've got to get down! The spacecraft is almost here!"

Josh paused for an instant, turned his head, and shot a glance high up in the sky. The spacecraft was a white ball of light, far up in the heavens. It was easy to see why everyone thought that it was a comet.

Josh climbed up a few more rungs and then stopped. He was about thirty feet off the ground, and the weird alien security guard was only a few feet below him.

Josh looked down, and I could tell what he was thinking. There was no way he could climb down now, and the spacecraft was almost directly above.

Josh was going to jump!

"No!" Rachel shrieked. "Don't do it, Josh! Don't do it!"

Time was running out. The white dot high in the sky slowed, and I knew that in seconds, a beam of high energy would come racing out of the sky and hit the antenna. But even if it didn't, the security guard was now right beneath Josh, reaching for his ankles.

And then Josh did the unthinkable. He turned, reached out with one hand—*and jumped from the antenna!*

27

"Josh!"

It was one word, but it came in three voices: mine, Rachel's, and Riley's. We all screamed at the same time, knowing that Josh would never survive the fall.

But Josh didn't *fall*.

He leapt, arms outstretched, and suddenly, he wasn't falling . . . he was *hanging!* He had jumped from the antenna . . . and grabbed one of the cables that supported the tower! He began to climb down the cable, swinging his legs from side to side as he drew one arm over the other and descended to the rooftop. He looked like he was a performer in a circus act.

Meanwhile, Mrs. Luchien wasn't going to hang around to see what happened. She spun on her heels, opened the door to the stairs, and stepped through. The door closed behind her. She was gone.

"She's getting away!" Riley shouted.

"Don't worry about her!" I shouted back. "We've got to help Josh!"

The three of us raced across the roof toward the antenna. Josh was still climbing down the cable, frantically trying to make it to the ground. The security guard was scrambling down the antenna, racing to make it back to the rooftop.

"You're almost there!" I shouted up to Josh. "Just a few more feet!"

Josh was still holding onto the cable, when I caught a movement up in the sky.

The tower was bending! The whole structure was bending, beginning at the place where Josh had loosened the bolts!

Riley screamed, and Rachel gasped. Josh, who was now only a few feet off the ground, let go of the cable. He dropped, fell to his knees, rolled, and got back up.

"The antenna!" I screamed, pointing upward. "It's . . . it's coming down!"

And it was. The antenna was leaning, farther and farther. We'd been able to loosen enough cables to make the towering structure become unsteady, and now the whole thing was coming down.

"*Oh no!*" Josh screamed. "*Not only is it coming down . . . but it's going to come down right on top of us!*"

28

The four of us ran like we'd never run before. The tower . . . that tall, spiraling metal antenna that had once pointed straight up into the sky like a flagpole . . . was tipping over.

Rachel and Riley ran one way, and Josh and I ran another. If we didn't get out of the way of the falling structure . . . .

No! I told myself. *Don't even think about it! Just run!*

And so that's what I did.

Behind me, I could hear the sounds of twisting metal, screeching and squealing as cables snapped and bars crunched.

Josh glanced over his shoulder. "Dive!" he shrieked, and immediately he was airborne, leaping forward like a frog. I did the same. Now I could hear a crashing sound behind me grow louder and louder. It sounded like a giant steel tree was falling over.

Josh hit the rubber roof first, and I landed right next to him, closed my eyes, and rolled. I rolled and rolled and rolled. The crashing sound grew louder, louder, louder still. I could hear the snapping metal as it crumbled down, crushing under its own weight.

Suddenly, an earth-shattering explosion filled my ears. It sounded like a bolt of lightning hitting metal and glass. The roof beneath me trembled and shook.

I rolled a few more times, then I opened my eyes. *The antenna had landed only a few feet away!*

"Holy cow!" Josh said, rolling once more and getting to his feet. "We almost got squished!"

I stood up. The antenna had snapped off right where Josh had loosened the bolts, leaving a twenty-foot lance pointing up into the sky. But the steel tower itself lay shattered on the roof. Cables that had once held the antenna firmly in place now snaked around the roof.

"Riley!" I shouted. "Rachel!"

"Over here!" I heard Rachel shout. "We're okay!"

Then I saw Rachel's head on the other side of the crumpled mass of metal that once was the tower. Riley's face popped into view, too.

We were all okay. It was a miracle, and the four of us had somehow escaped injury.

"Where's the security guard?" I asked.

We looked around, wary that he might be after us. I expected him to jump out from behind the wreckage of the tower and come after us, but he didn't.

Suddenly, Riley pointed and spoke. "I . . . I think that's him! Over there! Under the tower!"

We ran along the broken mass of steel and metal. Sure enough, the security guard was pinned under the wreckage.

But strangest of all . . . he was *smoking!* Smoke came out of his ears and his nose. There was a long gash on his arm . . . but no blood. The cut exposed hundreds of tiny wires and electrodes.

"He's . . . he's . . . a . . . a—" Rachel tried to get the words out, but she was too shocked.

"He's nothing but a robot!" I finished. I spun and looked at Josh. "That must mean—"

"I think you're right," Josh said, already knowing what I was thinking. "I think the aliens aren't really aliens at all. I think they're robots. Robots from outer space."

"Robots?!?!" Riley exclaimed. "But then, where do—"

Riley was interrupted by an ear-splitting blast and a blinding light. All four of us threw our hands to our faces, covering our eyes. When I spread a couple of my fingers to try and see, I gasped in horror.

A beam of light, twisting like a snake, was coming down from the sky! It stretched way up into the heavens like a glowing string of yarn.

But the problem was that the beam of light had connected with the stump of the antenna that still remained! The short part of the antenna was now fused with light!

"Oh no!" Josh exclaimed, and I could tell by his voice that our problems weren't over. "There's a chance that the energy beam is connecting to the apparatus below the mall! Come on! We've got to stop it somehow!"

He spun and Rachel, Riley, and I followed, racing after Josh. We climbed through the tangled wreckage of the fallen tower and sped toward the door. Josh reached it first, grabbed the handle, and pulled.

The door didn't budge.

"What's wrong?!?!" Rachel asked. "Open the door, Josh!"

Josh pulled harder and harder. There was a silver lever on the handle that didn't move.

"It . . . it's . . . it's—"

"Don't say it," Riley said. She covered her face with her hands. "Just don't say it," she repeated in despair.

"It's locked!" Josh suddenly blurted out.

Riley dropped her hands. "I told you *not* to say that!" she scolded.

Hope faded. The door—our only way out—was locked.

We were trapped on the roof.

29

Things were looking pretty hopeless. The door was locked, and we couldn't get off the roof. The only thing we could do was hope that the antenna had been permanently damaged and the energy beam from the spacecraft high above wouldn't reach the secret room deep beneath the mall.

The energy beam behind us suddenly went out, and we all turned. High above in the night sky, the alien spacecraft continued on its course.

"Maybe we can signal someone on the ground," Riley suggested. "You know . . . send out a signal for help somehow."

"That's a good idea," Josh said, "but we don't really have anything to signal with."

"Maybe someone saw that beam of light and they'll call the police," Rachel said.

Josh shook his head. "It's possible, but I don't think so," he said.

Then I had a worried thought.

"Hey Rachel," I said, "why haven't our parents come looking for us?" I asked. "I mean, we've been gone a long time."

Rachel shrugged. "I was thinking about that earlier," she replied. "I don't have any idea."

"Maybe the aliens ate them," Riley said.

"Yeah, right," I said with a frown.

"I'm sure we'll find out," Josh said. "Maybe your parents are looking for you right now. But mine . . . ."

He didn't have to say anything more. Josh's parents were beneath the mall, held captive and connected to the machine that was using their life energy. I felt bad for him. I didn't know where my mom and dad were, but they were probably safer than Josh's parents were.

We stood by the door, wondering what we could do. There were no stairs or other doors anywhere else on the roof. We didn't have any ropes, and the guide wires weren't long enough for us to use to climb down.

"Do you think that beam of energy made it all the way down to the secret room beneath the mall?" I asked.

"I don't know," Josh said. "We snapped the antenna, but the beam connected anyway. There's a chance—"

He stopped speaking. His eyes grew wide and lit up.

"Hey!" he said, snapping his fingers. "Jessica! That might be it!"

"What?" I asked.

"Yeah, what?" Rachel chimed in.

"To get the power to the apparatus in the cavern beneath the mall, the aliens are using energy beams, right?" Josh said excitedly. "Well, they're using the antenna to transfer the energy!"

"But we already knew that," Riley said.

"What I'm saying," Josh said, "is that I bet that tower—what's left of it—goes all the way through the mall—"

"—and down to the secret cavern!" I finished.

"Exactly!" Josh said. "That tower is wide! Maybe we can climb down it through the mall and take it all the way down!"

Josh sprinted across the rubber roof, heading toward the broken tower. The remaining piece still

145

pointed up into the sky. At the tip of it, jagged pieces of broken steel and metal splayed out, twisted and cracked from where the other part of the tower had snapped off.

At the base of the tower where it met the building was a dark hole. It was big . . . certainly big enough to get into. Problem was, the base of the tower was made with steel bars.

"There's no way we can get into the antenna," Riley said.

"Oh, yes there is," Josh replied, and he began searching the roof. "I need that wrench," he said. "I found it in a maintenance room near my dad's office. I dropped it just before I jumped from the antenna. Help me find it!"

We spread out and began searching for the wrench.

"Here it is!" Rachel said, bending over near the wreckage of the fallen tower. She stood up, waving the wrench above her head.

"Bring it here!" Josh said, running back to the base of the metal tower. Rachel sprinted up to Josh and handed him the tool. He went to work immediately, unscrewing bolts and unfastening rivets. Finally, he was able to pull one of the metal bars away, and then another. Soon, there was a space big enough to climb through.

"No more time to waste, guys," Josh said as he stuffed the wrench into his back pocket. "Let's hope we're right about this."

"What are we going to do?" Riley asked.

"We're climbing down, that's what we're doing," I replied. Riley looked frightened.

"It won't be that bad," Josh said. "We'll be climbing down through the inside of the tower. The metal bars are like the rungs of a ladder. You've climbed a ladder before, haven't you?" he asked.

Riley nodded.

"It'll be just like that, only it'll be dark," Josh said. "Come on."

And with that, Josh ducked down between the metal and grasped a rung. It looked like he was climbing down a mine shaft. I followed. Riley was next, followed by Rachel.

We were on our way. Whether or not the antenna would take us all the way to the secret cavern . . . well, we didn't know.

But we were about to find out.

Climbing down the tower wasn't that difficult. There were plenty of metal rungs to grab onto, but it was very, very dark. It was so dark we couldn't even see one another.

"Whatever you do, don't let go," Josh said from below me.

"Don't worry, I won't" Riley said from above.

Down we climbed, down, down, into the depths of the mall. It felt like we were going to the center of the earth.

"How are we going to know when we reach the bottom?" Rachel asked.

"I don't have any idea," Josh said. "This tower might not even go all the way to the cavern. But it has to go somewhere."

"And somehow it has to connect to that huge machine," I said.

"Right," Josh agreed.

"It feels like we've gone a million miles," Riley complained.

"We've gone a long way, that's for sure," Josh said in the darkness below me. "But I think we're getting close. I can hear a noise below us."

We all stopped climbing. Josh was right! I could hear a rumbling sound coming from beneath us. It was a mechanical whirring noise that sounded like the hum of a large machine.

We started climbing down again. Five minutes later, I heard a metal thud below me.

"End of the line," Josh said. I climbed down two more rungs and bumped into Josh. Then Rachel was beside us, followed by Riley.

We were inside of the base of the tower, and there wasn't much room for the four of us. The mechanical whirring sound drummed loudly in our ears.

"How do we get out of here?" I asked.

"There has to be some kind of panel or door," Josh replied. "Let's see if we can find it."

Using our hands, we felt all along the metal rungs. I could feel what felt like wires and knobs, but nothing that resembled a door.

"Hold on, hold on," Josh said. "I think there's something here."

I could hear Josh fumbling with something in the darkness. Then there was a *click* sound, and suddenly a slice of light lit up our tiny area.

It was a door!

"You did it, Josh!" Riley exclaimed.

"Shhhh," he replied. *"I don't know where we are. We have to be careful."*

"Well, let's get out of here," Rachel said. "I'm getting all cramped up in here."

"Not so fast," Josh replied. "Let's have a look."

Josh opened the door a tiny crack. Rachel, Riley, and I huddled close to peer through the small opening.

What we saw made all four of us gasp. Riley was so freaked out that she backed away and threw her hands to her face. Rachel, Josh and I could do nothing but stare.

We were in the cavern, all right. The huge machine was directly in front of us. On the other side were rows and rows of people . . . the ones we had seen earlier when we'd been captured. They were still hooked up to all of those wires.

But now, on the other side of the room, were rows of mannequins. They hadn't been there earlier. They all stood in the same position, still and unmoving. Each mannequin was connected to a set of wires that ran up along the ceiling and down into the machine in the center of the huge cavern.

"Oh no!" Josh hissed. *"I think we're too late! Look!"*

Josh pointed, and I gasped again.

In the middle of the cavern, near the giant machine, was Mrs. Luchien. She had her hand on a large lever. There were a few other mannequins around her. Some of them were working at computer screens and fiddling with buttons and knobs on control panels.

"We now have the energy we need!" Mrs. Luchien was saying. "Now, we can continue with our plan! Nothing will stop us, and we will take over the world!"

And then, without warning, Mrs. Luchien pulled the lever down.

31

Suddenly, lights on the giant machine began to blink. A large wheel near the top began to spin like a merry-go-round. It started slow, but was rapidly picking up speed.

"It won't be long now!" Mrs. Luchien shouted above the growing noise.

"Do something, Josh!" I whispered. *"We've got to stop them!"*

Josh shook his head. "I don't know what we can do," he replied helplessly.

Behind us, Riley was still backed against the inside of the tower, her hands over her face. *"This isn't happening,"* she was saying quietly. *"This is all a bad dream. It's a bad dream, and I'm going to wake up."*

Oh, how I wished she was right! It would be great if all four of us would wake up, only to find out that this whole thing had been a nightmare.

But that wasn't going to happen, and I knew it.

"Maybe if we can get to that lever, we can shut the machine down," Rachel whispered.

"Yeah, but we'd get caught for sure," I replied.

Josh was studying the machine, watching the big metal wheel on top of it spin round and round, faster and faster.

"Get ready to transfer the energy!" Mrs. Luchien shouted.

"See that rotating wheel?" Josh asked.

"Yeah?" I replied.

"I think that's how the energy is being transformed. It's being changed in the machine so that it's more than just electrical energy, and when that wheel gets moving fast enough, it will send the energy to the mannequins over there."

"But what will that do to the humans over on the other side?" Rachel asked, nodding toward the large group of people that were grouped together.

Josh heaved a resigned sigh. He didn't answer. He didn't have to. If we didn't stop the machine, it would be all over . . . for all of us.

"There's only one thing I can try," Josh said. "I don't know if it will work."

"Any idea is better than nothing," I replied.

"It's risky," he said.

"I don't care," I answered.

"And it'll be dangerous," he said.

"Josh!" I exclaimed. "I don't care! We have to stop them!"

"Okay then," he said. "Here's the plan. Mrs. Luchien and the mannequins are all facing the other way, right?"

I glanced around the large cavern.

"Yeah," I said.

"Well, you and Rachel and Riley sneak over there." He pointed toward the far side of the cavern. "Meanwhile, I'll sneak up as close as I can to the machine." He pointed to the whirling wheel atop the apparatus.

"Yeah, but then what are you going to do?" Rachel asked.

Josh pulled out the wrench that he'd been carrying in his back pocket.

"Let's just say I'm going to try and throw a wrench in their plans," he said. "Are you ready?"

I nodded, and so did Rachel. Riley nodded too.

"You guys head over there. When you see me get close to the machine, make a lot of noise to attract the attention of Mrs. Luchien and the dummies. Hopefully, that will give me enough time to get close enough."

The plan was risky, that was for sure. Would it work?

We were about to find out.

32

Josh pushed the small door open and the four of us exited the tiny space. Thankfully, the noise from the giant machine in the middle of the cavern was so loud that it would conceal any noise that we might make. Nevertheless, we would still have to be careful. We couldn't afford to be spotted until we were on the other side of the cave and Josh was in position.

"Good luck," I whispered to Josh. He nodded and quickly began tiptoeing across the floor toward the contraption.

Rachel, Riley and I headed toward the other side of the room. I kept glancing back at Mrs. Luchien and the mannequins, hoping that they wouldn't see us. Thankfully, they seemed to be too involved in watching the strange apparatus, waiting for the energy to begin transferring from the machine to the hundreds of motionless dummies that lined the far wall.

And on the other side of the cavern, still connected to those wires, were humans. I felt bad for them. They hadn't done anything wrong. They were just at the wrong place at the wrong time.

Maybe it wasn't too late to save them.

Maybe.

We reached the corner of the cavern. There was a stack of metal plates and what looked to be a giant air conditioner in the corner, which was perfect. It gave us a place to hide while Josh got closer to the machine.

We ducked into the shadows and hunkered down. Across the cavern, that strange wheel kept whirling and whirling. Josh was tiptoeing closer and closer.

Suddenly, he stopped, turned and looked back at us. He nodded. With one hand he drew back the wrench, and with the other he gave us a thumbs up.

He was ready.

"That's his signal!" I whispered. "Let's make some noise!"

The three of us leapt from our hiding place and into the open.

"Hey, you goofy dummies!" I shouted, jumping up and down into the air. "Look where we are!"

Mrs. Luchien snapped her head around. The mannequins turned, surprised by the sudden noise.

"Yah! Yah! Yah!" Riley shouted, doing a little dance.

"Hey, you silly alien-mannequins!" Rachel shouted.

Mrs. Luchien threw out her arm and pointed an accusing finger at us. "Get them! Now!" she shouted.

Suddenly, the mannequins that had been around the giant machine began coming toward us. They moved slow and machine-like, but it wouldn't be long before they reached us.

Out of the corner of my eye I saw Josh move. The mannequins hadn't spotted him, and now he was able to get right up to the large apparatus in the middle of the cavern. His arm was still cocked back, gripping the wrench.

Suddenly, Mrs. Luchien spotted him.

"No!" she screeched. The mannequins that were heading toward us stopped and turned.

"What are you doing?!?!" Mrs. Luchien cried out, her eyes wide. She began to run toward Josh—but it was too late.

Josh took aim, drew his arm back farther, then let the wrench fly. I had no idea what was about to happen.

The only thing we could do now was hope.

The wrench tumbled and spun through the air, arcing up high, then coming down, down, down—

Clang!

It landed right in the middle of the spinning metal wheel!

There was an awful screech, and the sound of grinding metal. Then there was an explosion and a plume of smoke snaked up, followed by a ton of sparks. Lights on the machine blinked on and off. A warning siren blared.

"No!" Mrs. Luchien screamed again. She ran back to the machine and began flipping switches and dials.

All of a sudden, the big metal wheel stopped with a lurching halt. There was another explosion, and more sparks bloomed out, showering the cavern floor. A deep, heavy rumble began to growl from within the large machine.

"This cannot happen!" Mrs. Luchien shouted above the noise. She was still frantically flipping switches and dials. I think she was trying to turn the machine off.

Josh had run back to the tower door, and now he sprinted to where we were. The mannequins paid no attention to us now, as they were all too busy attending to the sputtering machine.

"What's going to happen?" Riley asked.

Josh shrugged. "Your guess is as good as mine," he said. "But we need to help all of those people over there! My mom and dad and sister are there somewhere!"

Rows and rows of humans were still connected to the wires that were connected to the machine. None of them were moving, and I hoped that it wasn't too late.

And then:

The rumbling from within the machine grew so loud that it hurt my head. I threw my hands up over my ears, and so did Josh, Riley, and Rachel.

All at once there was a loud explosion and a bright light. A sudden surge of power streamed up into the electrical wires on the ceiling. The wires glowed hot yellow, and tiny bulges of energy followed the wires like trains on tracks. The volts sped along the thin cables, twisting and turning . . . and connected with the hundreds of lifeless mannequins that were attached to the apparatus.

And what happened next was unbelievable.

34

All at once, every single mannequin that was hooked up to the wires—the ones that Mrs. Luchien was trying to bring to life—*exploded!*

There was plastic flying everywhere. A plastic foot flew over my head and bounced off the wall. A plastic hand landed by my feet. It was really kind of gross, even though I knew it was only plastic.

And then something else happened.

All of the humans that had been connected to the wires began to move. Slowly, I could see their heads begin to nod from side to side. Fingers began to twitch. One by one, the humans began to pull the metal ringlets from their fingers and disconnect themselves from the wires.

Meanwhile, Mrs. Luchien stood by the large contraption in the middle of the cavern. Around her, the mannequins were falling to their knees, then dropping to the floor.

"What's happening to them?" Riley asked.

"I think we just destroyed their energy supply," Josh said. "Look."

As we watched, more mannequins fell. But perhaps best of all, Mrs. Luchien seemed to be losing control. She acted like a robot that was low on batteries. She tried to speak, but no sound came out.

"She's a robot, too!" Rachel exclaimed.

And she was. Mrs. Luchien suddenly fell to the ground . . . and her arm fell off! Wires came out of her shoulder! Sparks and smoke came out of her ears. It was one of the freakiest things I had ever seen in my life.

More and more humans were moving, but they seemed . . . different. It appeared that they were waking up or coming back to life, only not all the way. As we watched, several of the humans began to walk, robot-like, toward the door that led up to the first level.

Then, Josh recognized his dad!

"Dad!" he exclaimed, running up to him. *"Dad! It's me!"*

But Josh's dad didn't even blink. He just kept walking toward the door in a trance-like state, his eyes all glossy. He didn't even recognize his own son!

I began to think that maybe we'd really screwed things up, after all.

"Dad! Dad!" Josh pleaded. *"Talk to me! Say something!"*

But Josh's dad acted like he didn't even hear him. He walked right on past, heading toward the door with all of the other people.

"Let's go upstairs!" Josh said. "We've got to figure out what's happened!"

We walked to the door amidst the streaming crowd of people. My mind spun, and I could tell that Rachel and Riley and Josh were just as worried as I was. Suppose these humans never returned to their normal selves? What would happen if they stayed like this forever?

I couldn't bear the thought.

We walked silently up the stairs. Not one person spoke. The only sound we heard was the sound of people walking up the steps.

In a few moments we came to the first level and emerged from the secret door in the LEGO Imagination Center. People poured out, but they just walked aimlessly around the dark mall. Even Josh's dad acted like a robot. It was pretty scary.

Then Josh recognized his mom. He went up to her and tried to get her to talk, but the result was the same as it had been with his father. Josh's mom acted like he wasn't even there.

"What have we done?!?!" he said frantically, looking around at the zombie-like people. "What have we done?!?!"

"It's almost like that machine still has power over them," I said.

Josh froze. He gasped.

"Jess! That's it!"

"Huh?" I said. "What?"

"That machine! We stopped it from transferring the energy to the mannequins . . . but it still has control over their minds! We have to completely destroy it!"

"You think that'll work?" Rachel asked.

"It's the only chance we've got!" Josh replied. He ran past us. "Come on! Come on!"

We sprang after him. We went back through the secret door and flew down the stairs. Our footsteps echoed down the narrow staircase.

I didn't know exactly how we were going to shut down the huge machine . . . but as it turned out, we had a bigger problem.

A *much* bigger problem.

When we reached the bottom of the stairs, Josh pulled the door open.

Suddenly, he was attacked . . . *by a plastic hand!* It grabbed him by the throat and wouldn't let go!

Suddenly, we all came under attack from strange, plastic hands, and I realized what had happened. Although the mannequins themselves had been destroyed, parts of them were still under the control of the giant machine! Hands and feet were everywhere.

And when a plastic hand suddenly leapt up from the ground and grasped my neck, I knew that all four of us would never stand a chance.

35

Plastic hands and feet were everywhere, attacking from all directions. They leapt up from the ground and swarmed like angry bees. A plastic mannequin hand gripped my throat, while a plastic foot kicked me in the shin.

Somehow, I managed to pull the hand from my throat. As soon as I did, another one attacked, but I was able to knock it away.

"The machine!" Josh gasped, struggling to pull the plastic hand from his neck. "It still has control!"

I had been able to free myself first, so I bounded past Rachel, Riley and Josh and ran to the gigantic machine in the center of the cavern.

"The computer terminal!" Josh shouted. He had fallen to his knees and was still struggling frantically, trying to pull the insane plastic hand from his throat. "Smash the computer terminal, Jess! Smash it to bits!"

I ran over to the large computer terminal. It was making whirring noises, and lights were blinking on and off.

How am I going to smash this thing? I thought. My mind was racing. I looked around for something I could use, but I found nothing.

Meanwhile, more and more plastic hands and feet were attacking. There were hundreds of them! I had to keep swatting them away and kicking them aside. One hand landed on my shoulder, its fingers grabbing my ears. I yanked it away and thought my entire ear was going to come off. It really hurt.

Something grabbed my ankles, and I was horrified to see Mrs. Luchien's plastic arm. The hand held my leg in a vice-like grip. I tried to shake it away, but it was no use.

"Hurry, Jess, hurry!" Rachel shouted. I looked over at my friends. There were hands all over them. This was one battle that they weren't going to win. If I couldn't shut down the main computer terminal, we were all goners.

The grip around my leg was painful. I picked up a chair and slammed it down on the plastic arm . . . and it let go. I pulled my leg away and smashed the chair down again.

Crunch! The chair fell apart in my hand, leaving me with one long piece of the back of the chair.

It was all I needed.

I ran to the computer terminal, raised the back of the chair high above my head . . . and brought it down on top of the computer.

36

The effect of the back of the chair hitting the main computer terminal was immediate.

There was a loud crash as the metal in my hand struck the metal console. Glass shattered. Lights stopped blinking.

I brought the metal chair over my head again, but a plastic hand jumped up from the terminal and found my throat. I jerked it away with my free hand and tossed it to the floor. Then I stepped on it.

I brought the metal chair down onto the terminal again.

Crash!

The terminal seemed to explode. More glass broke, and smoke began to hiss out.

But most importantly, the large unit looked like it was dying. Even the plastic hands and feet that had attacked with such fury seemed to be slowing down, like they were getting weaker and weaker.

"Jessica!" Rachel shouted. "You're doing it!"

I turned quickly and caught a glimpse of my friends. They were still battling the plastic hands and feet.

"Don't stop now, Jess!" Josh shouted. I turned to the computer terminal, brought the back of the chair over my head, and brought it down as hard as I could.

The lights blinked off. A motor whined to a stop. Smoke continued to billow out from the sides of the terminal, but the machine itself had stopped working. The floor was covered with plastic hands and feet. Some of them were still twitching, but they no longer seemed to have a life of their own.

Rachel, Riley and Josh cheered from behind me. I turned to see them running up to me, no longer fighting the vicious hands and feet that had been attacking from everywhere.

"You did it!" Riley exclaimed, her brown hair bouncing around her face. "You did it, Jessica!"

"Let's go back upstairs and see if that's changed my mom and dad!" Josh replied hopefully.

The four of us ran to the door and sprinted up the steps. For the first time in a while, I realized that I was exhausted. It had been a long night, but it seemed like we had been running for days.

We reached the first level of the mall. Everything was still very, very dark, and just as eerie as it had been earlier.

But not a single person was in sight.

"Where . . . where did everyone go?" Riley asked, turning her head from side to side. It was really odd that so many people seemed to have vanished.

"They've got to be here somewhere!" Rachel said. "There had to have been hundreds of people in that cavern!"

"Let's split up," Josh said. "We'll have a better chance of finding someone if we all head out in different directions."

"Yeah, but what if there are other mannequins still around?" I asked.

"Good point," Josh said. "Let's pair up then. Rachel and Riley . . . you two head toward Macy's, and then up to North Garden. Jessica and I will head toward Bloomingdale's, past Underwater Adventures, and we'll meet you in the North Gardens."

Riley and Rachel headed out, and Josh and I went in the opposite direction.

"Do you really think we got rid of all the mannequins?" I asked Josh.

He nodded. "Yeah, I think we did. I don't understand why we can't find anyone, but I think all of those freaky mannequins are gone."

Josh was wrong . . . and in five seconds, we were about to find out how wrong he was.

37

Josh and I walked quickly, keeping an eye out for any of the people that had emerged from the cavern.

"See anything yet?" I asked, looking around. The mall seemed abandoned.

Josh shook his head. "Nope," he said.

We reached Bloomingdale's Court and turned, heading north past Underwater Adventures. Underwater Adventures is a really cool place. It has gigantic aquariums filled with all kinds of fish . . . even sharks!

But tonight everything was dark, and there was nothing to see — until I caught a movement out of the corner of my eye.

I grabbed Josh's arm, and we stopped.

"Over there!" I whispered. *"There's someone over there!"*

We had been headed north, and we were half way between Bloomingdale's and Sears. There is a rotunda area with escalators, elevators, telephone booths, and restrooms.

"Where did you see it?" Josh whispered.

"Over by the elevator," I answered.

We hurried over to the elevator, and were caught by surprise when the doors suddenly slid open.

I gasped. Josh gasped.

There, on the elevator, were mannequins.

Not one. Not two.

But five or six.

They just stood there, frozen, bathed in an eerie light that came from the elevator.

And suddenly, one of them moved. He was wearing blue pants and a blue shirt. He looked like he was a maintenance man.

"For crying out loud," he said, pushing aside other mannequins and stepping out of the elevator. "For the life of me, I don't know how all of these things got here. Especially during a fire drill. How come you kids are still in here?"

"Fire drill?" I said.

"Yep. We're having a fire drill at this very moment. You two should be outside."

I looked at Josh and he looked at me.

"Let's go!" I said excitedly. We spun and ran, up past Sears and through the North Gardens. Rachel and Riley had just arrived, and it looked like they had been running.

And Rachel was carrying our backpacks! She must have stopped at the department store where we'd dropped them earlier.

"Outside!" Josh exclaimed. "Everyone's outside!"

"We know!" Riley said, and the four of us ran to the exit doors.

"Here, Jessica," Rachel said, handing me my backpack as we ran. "I picked it up at the department store."

"Thanks," I said, and I took the backpack from her and slung it over my shoulder as I ran. In seconds, the four of us reached the doors, pushed them open, and burst outside.

The night air was chilly. Bright lights lit up the parking lot, and there were people milling about all over the place. Some of them were talking with one another, and some were laughing. I recognized a few of them from the cavern.

"You're free!" I said to a woman with long hair. She gave me a strange glance.

"What do you mean?" she asked.

"You're free! You're free from the aliens! From the mannequins!"

Again, she gave me another strange look, then she burst out laughing.

"Yes, of course, dear," she said, and walked away.

"Josh . . . what's going on?" I whispered. "Didn't she realize what she's just been through?"

Suddenly, Josh spotted his parents and his sister.

"Mom! Dad!" he shouted. He took off running toward them, and I followed.

"There you are," Dad said. "We've been looking for you. Ready to go home?"

"Huh?" Josh said. "What do you mean?"

"It's almost nine o'clock," Josh's father said. "We've got to get going. Say good-bye to your friend, and we'll see you at the car. It's parked right over there."

Josh just stood there, his mouth open wide.

"Do you think anyone here realizes what just happened?" I whispered to Josh.

He shook his head. "It doesn't look like it," he replied. "But I think everyone will know soon enough. Especially when they find the broken tower on the roof."

"And the weird contraption in the secret cavern below the mall," I said.

And then I was struck with an awful thought.

"My mom and dad!" I said. "They're going to be furious!"

The 'fire drill' appeared to be over, and people began streaming back into the mall. I pushed my way through the crowd, found a pay phone just beyond the doors, and called home.

"Hello?" Mom answered.

"Mom! It's me! Don't worry! I'm at the Mall of America, and I'm fine."

There was a pause, then Mom spoke. "I know you are, honey," she said. "You called and asked if you could stay at the mall and then spend the night at Rachel's."

"I did?" I said.

"Yes. Don't you remember?"

"Uh . . . well . . . um, yeah. I . . . I guess I did. Well . . . uh . . . plans have changed. Can you come and get me?"

"Yes," Mom replied. "But you sound different. Is anything wrong?"

I thought for a moment. "No," I replied. "Nothing's wrong. It's just been a really weird night. I'll explain when you get here."

I found Rachel by the drinking fountain. She looked at me and shook her head.

"I just talked to my mom," she said. "She said that I called her to say that I was spending the night at your house!"

I gasped. "My mom said the same thing!" I exclaimed.

"Do you suppose that somehow the aliens did that? You know . . . like Josh had said happened to him. The aliens had called his school and told them that they were moving. I bet they did that so no one would get suspicious."

"I suppose," I said. "After tonight, I'd believe just about anything."

But the strangeness wasn't over, as I would find out the very next morning.

38

I was so glad when I awoke the next morning in my very own bed. Mom had picked me up at the mall the night before. I tried to explain to her what happened, but when I said the word 'alien' and 'spacecraft', she just laughed.

"Jessica, really," she had said. "You and your wild imagination. You really ought to put down your ideas in a book."

I didn't even try to explain further. I knew that there was no way she would believe me.

I got up and peeled an orange for breakfast. Mom and Dad were in the living room having coffee, watching the television. My brother Mark had already left for school. He's on the swim team, and they practice really early in the morning.

"Some pretty strange things happened at the mall last night," Dad said. "Did you see anything?"

"Nothing except mannequins that came to life," I said. "Oh. And a spacecraft that shot down a beam of energy into an antenna."

I expected Dad to laugh, but he pointed to the television. "They just showed the tower," he said. "They said that lightning hit it."

I sat down and watched TV while I ate my orange. On the news, lots of people at the Mall of America were being interviewed. Some were saying that they couldn't remember what had happened. Yet others said that they had found strange things around the mall. One of the security guards said that somehow all of the mannequins in the entire mall had been picked up and put in different places.

"Did you see anything like that?" Dad asked.

"Oh, sure," I replied. "We saw mannequins all over the place." I knew that if I told him about everything we went through he would think that I lost my mind.

But I had to know. Just for the sake of my own sanity, I had to know if what Rachel, Riley, Josh and I had been through was real.

And I knew what I had to do.

The very next weekend, Mom dropped me off at the Mall of America. She said she'd pick me up in an hour. Rachel's mom dropped her off, too, and we met at the North Garden.

"If what happened to us was real," I told her, "that giant machine will still be in that secret cavern. Let's go check it out."

The mall was really busy, and there were people all over the place as we made our way to the LEGO Imagination Center. Oddly enough, a man was coming out of the door in the floor. When we tried to go through the door and down the stairs, he stopped us.

"Sorry girls," he said, holding his hand up. "That's off limits."

"What's down there?" I asked.

"Oh, that's just one of the furnace rooms," the man said. "Nothing at all to see down there."

Furnace room? I thought. *That's what was down there?!?!*

"But . . . but isn't there a bunch of mannequin parts down there?" Rachel asked.

The man shook his head. "No, not down there. The only thing down there is the furnace."

Rachel and I looked at each other and shrugged. There were a lot of things that we just couldn't explain, but there was one thing for sure: all four of us had experienced the same thing. Rachel, Riley, Josh and I knew the truth. However bizarre it sounded, however creepy it had been, it had been true. I was sure that what I had been through was the creepiest thing I'd ever heard.

That is, until we went on a vacation to visit my aunt and uncle in Indiana.

We go there twice a year and stay for a weekend. My Uncle Jack and Aunt Barb live in Elkhart, Indiana. It's a city in the northern part of the state. They live near the St. Joseph river and we have a lot of fun. Plus, I've met a lot of new friends there.

The day we arrived was cloudy, and it looked like it might rain. It was October, so it was a little chilly. I put on my jacket and decided to walk across the street to see if my friend, Travis Hall, was home. I've known Travis my whole life. I only wish that I got to see him more than twice a year.

He came to the door when I knocked.

"Hey Jess!" he said. "I didn't know you guys were coming down this weekend!"

"We're here until Sunday," I said.

"Cool!" he exclaimed. "Come on in."

We were going to go down to the river, but it started to rain. Plus, it got cold, so we stayed indoors. We were playing a game of checkers when I decided to tell him what happened to us at the Mall of America. So far, no one I had told the story to would believe me. Most people just laughed and said that I was making it up. After a while, I stopped telling people about it. But I thought Travis might like to hear the story.

When I finished telling him all about the spacecraft and the mannequins and Mrs. Luchien and the secret cavern below the mall, Travis just stared with his mouth open.

"You're not kidding, are you?" he said.

I shook my head. "No. I'm serious. It really happened. You believe me?"

He nodded. "I'll believe your story if you believe the one I'm going to tell you," he said.

"About aliens?" I asked.

He shook his head, and his black hair swished on his forehead. "No, not aliens. Worse."

"What could be worse than aliens from outer space?" I asked.

"Insects," he said matter-of-factly.

"Insects?!?!" I said. "You mean . . . like . . . *bugs*?"

Travis nodded.

"What's the big deal about insects?" I asked.

"Oh, these weren't just any insects," he replied. "These insects were made of *iron*. They were the scariest things I've ever seen."

"Iron insects?!?!" I exclaimed. I tried to imagine what they would look like.

"Yep," Travis said. "If I tell you the truth, will you laugh at me?"

"Of course not!" I said. And I meant it.

"Okay, then I'll tell you everything that happened."

And with that, Travis sat back in his chair, folded his arms, and told me about the terrifying things that had happened to him . . . .

Next:

#9: Iron Insects Invade Indiana

Continue on for a FREE preview!

1

"Gotcha!"

Although I recognized the voice instantly, I was still surprised by the tight hands grasping my waist. I jumped and dropped my water balloon that I had been filling up at the spigot on the outside of our house. It exploded when it hit the grass, spraying cold water all over my bare legs and feet.

I spun.

Just as I expected, there stood Mandy McKinley, my neighbor from across the street. If it had been anyone else that had surprised me like that, I would have been mad. Especially since it had cost me a balloon.

But it was Mandy. One of my very best friends.

"You made me waste a balloon," I said, frowning.

Mandy shrugged and dug into the pocket of her denim cutoffs. She pulled out a handful of balloons.

"Where did you get those?!" I gasped.

"I swiped them from Eddie Finkbinder," she replied with a crafty smirk.

My jaw dropped. Eddie Finkbinder was nothing but a bully. If he knew that Mandy had swiped his balloons, he'd be furious.

"You're kidding!" I exclaimed.

"Nope!" Mandy replied. "He owes them to you, anyway. So it wasn't like I stole them. I just got back the ones that he took from you."

Mandy was right. Last week I had a brand-new bag of balloons that I was going to fill with water. I left them on my porch when I was mowing the back lawn, and Eddie swiped them. I knew he did because I saw him with them a few days later. Plus, he was bragging to all of his friends that he'd taken them.

Problem is, Eddie is in seventh grade. I'm only in fifth, and Eddie is a lot bigger than me. I think just about everyone on our block is afraid of Eddie Finkbinder.

Myself included.

But what was going to happen to Mandy and me later that day would be a lot scarier than Eddie Finkbinder.

In fact, now that I think about it, what was about to happen would scare the daylights out of anyone . . . and it all started with a simple trip to the river.

My name is Travis Kramer, and I live in Elkhart, Indiana. I think Elkhart is one of the coolest places to live on the planet. We live near the St. Joseph River, and there's lots of things to do all year round. Among other things, Elkhart is known as the 'band instrument capital of the world'. As a matter of fact, my dad works at a factory that makes musical instruments.

But in the summertime, my favorite thing to do is go to hang out by the river . . . that is, when I'm not having water balloon fights with my friends.

And that's what Mandy and I had planned for this particular day. The sun was out, the temperature was warm, and it would be a perfect afternoon for swimming, Frisbee, and just plain having fun in the water.

We rode our bikes to a park by the St. Joseph River. It's not very far from where we live. Lots of other people go there, too, especially on the really hot days.

When we got there, I spread out my blanket on the grass, and Mandy spread hers out next to mine.

"Want to catch frogs?" I asked her.

She shook her head. "Nah. I'm going to swim for a while."

And with that she jumped up, kicked off her sandals, and ran through the hot sand. She plunged head first into the cool, blue water.

I took off my sneakers and walked down to the shore. There were a few other people milling about in the water and along the shore. Mostly little kids with their parents.

I walked along the shoreline. Not far away, the swimming area ends and tall cattails grow on the shore and in the water. It's one of the best places I know of to catch frogs.

Sure enough, I spotted one right away. A big, fat leopard frog. Leopard frogs are bright green with black spots . . . that's how they got their name. They're really fast, too . . . but I'm faster.

I froze. Then, I slowly leaned forward, reaching out with my arms. The trick is to move real slow so the frog doesn't know you're going to grab him. When your hand is in reach—*zappo!* You reach out and catch him.

I was just about to lunge when I felt something on my arm. I barely noticed it at first, but then it felt heavier. I was sure it was some kind of bug, but if I swatted it now, I would scare the frog.

But suddenly it scratched my skin! The bug felt heavy, and I stood straight up and slapped at my arm. I was sure that it was a huge bee or maybe a hornet.

But that's not what it was.

When I smacked it, the insect buzzed off, but it didn't go very far. It landed on a cattail reed only a few feet away.

And I couldn't believe my eyes.

"Holy smokes!" I said quietly.

Right then and there I knew that this wasn't going to be just another day at the park.

2

I forgot all about the frog. What I was looking at made me forget about everything.

The insect—the bug that had landed on my arm—was all shiny and silver. It was kind of big, too . . . about the size of a Matchbox car.

As I watched, it crawled up the stem of the cattail. The insect was so heavy that it bent the stalk. I wasn't sure what kind if insect it was, either. It looked like it might be a locust. But then again, there's no locust I know of that's made of metal!

The creature moved slow and methodical, robot-like, until it reached the top of the cattail. By now the plant was almost completely bent over from the weight of the insect.

Then, without warning, the insect flew. It came right at me and I ducked just as it went by my ear. Its wings drummed the air like a tiny airplane motor. I turned and watched it as it buzzed up into the air, then swooped around and disappeared into the trees.

I stood in the water for a moment, wondering if there might be any more. That was the freakiest thing I'd ever seen! Maybe there really *was* such a thing as insects made out of metal.

Or, maybe it's not metal at all, I thought. *Maybe it just* looked *like metal.*

No. I know what I saw.

A few minutes passed, and I still hadn't spotted any more of the bizarre insects.

I've got to tell Mandy about this, I thought, and I turned around and sloshed through the water back to the swimming area.

Mandy was on her towel. She had her sunglasses on, and she was reading a book.

"You're not going to believe what I found!" I exclaimed.

"A frog," she said without interest, not looking up from her book.

"Better!" I said excitedly. I plopped down on my towel.

"Okay," she said, turning a page. "You found a turtle."

"I saw a bug!" I said.

She looked up at me like I was crazy. "So what?" she said.

"Mandy . . . the bug was made out of steel or something! Honest!"

At this, she placed the book in her lap and lowered her sunglasses.

"I think you've been out in the sun too long," she said.

"Mandy, I'm not kidding! It was a real, live insect of some sort . . . only it was made out of metal! It was shiny and silver like a pop can."

Mandy's frown faded.

"You're . . . you're serious?" she asked.

I nodded. "No tricks. I wouldn't have believed it myself if I hadn't seen it."

"Are there any more?" she asked.

"I didn't see any." I turned and pointed. "It was over there, where the swimming area ends. Over where the cattails grow."

Mandy leapt up. "Let's go see if there are any more!" she exclaimed.

We had just started out across the grass . . . but we didn't get far. The scream of a little girl caused us to stop in our tracks.

"He's going to bite me!" she shrieked. *"He's going to bite me! Help! Help!"*

"It's one of those nasty insects!" I said. "Come on! We've got to help her before it bites her!"

We sprinted across the grass, and we could only hope to get to the little girl before the awful insect stung.

3

Thankfully, the little girl wasn't far away. Her mother was close by, too, and she was there before we were.

"What is it?" the woman exclaimed frantically. With one quick motion, she swept up her frantic daughter in her arms.

Safe with her mom, the little girl turned and pointed.

"Bad!" she said. "Bad, bad!"

We ran up to them.

"What is it?" I asked. My eyes scanned the ground.

"Bad!" the little girl said again, still pointing at the grass.

"Oh, for goodness sake," Mandy whispered in my ear. *"Look, Travis."* She pointed.

On the ground near her towel was a toad.

That's it.

A plain, ordinary toad, no bigger than the palm of my hand.

"Sweetheart," the little girl's mother said, "toad's don't bite. Toads are our friends."

"Bad!" the little girl shouted defiantly.

The mother turned to us. "I'm sorry we disturbed you," she said. "But thank you just the same."

"Hey, no problem," I said. "I'm just glad she's all right."

Mandy and I turned and walked back to our blankets. Mandy started snickering.

"I can't believe she was freaked out by a toad," she said. "When I was her age, I was catching them and putting them in a shoe box."

"Me too," I said with a laugh.

We walked across the grass and over to where the marsh begins. We searched and searched, but we didn't see any more of the strange, silvery insects.

"I'm telling you, I know what I saw," I said.

"I believe you, Travis," Mandy said. "I just wish that I could see one, too."

After an hour of looking, we gave up. I was really disappointed, and I was sure that I probably wouldn't ever see another one of those insects again in my life.

Which, of course, wasn't going to be the case . . . because it just so happened that I *would* see another one.

Not only would I *see* it, but I would *catch* it.

And *that's* what got me into serious trouble.

4

A few days went by, and I didn't think too much more about the strange insect at the river. I guess I just figured that it was one of those once-in-a-lifetime opportunities, and I wouldn't get a chance to see one up close again.

Whatever it was.

One afternoon I was in the garage working on my skateboard. It's one that I built from a kit, and it's really cool. I give it a tune-up once in a while to keep the wheel bearings in good shape. It's a fast skateboard, I can tell you that much. My friends will, too.

Suddenly, I noticed a strange clapping noise. The clapping sound was really rapid, like—

Wings.

The garage door was open. Dad was at work, so his car was gone.

And while I watched, a large, shiny insect swooped up from the driveway, arced down, and landed in the very spot that Dad parks his car. The creature came to a rest on the cement, and just sat there. Like the insect I had found at the lake, this one, too, was all silvery and shiny, and about the size of a Matchbox car.

I was overcome with excitement. I had given up on ever seeing one of the unusual bugs again, but now there was one in my very own garage!

I didn't move a muscle for fear of scaring him away. So I just stood there, looking at him.

And there was no question what this one was, either.

It was a grasshopper. No doubt about it. I could see his long, bent legs and his two giant eyes.

A silver grasshopper.

And the longer I watched, the more excited I became. The more I realized that no one would believe that I had spotted such an insect unless I could show it to them.

So I began to think of a way to catch the little bugger.

I turned slowly and looked for some sort of container. The only thing that was in reach was an old mayonnaise jar on the workbench. It was filled with nuts and bolts that Dad had been saving.

That would have to work. I leaned over the desk and grasped the jar without taking my eyes away from the shiny insect on the garage floor. I unscrewed the lid. As gently as I could, I emptied the nuts and bolts onto the workbench. They clanked against the glass jar and thumped on the wood, but the grasshopper in the garage didn't seem to care.

Then, with the jar in my left hand and the lid in my right, I began to tiptoe slowly toward the insect.

As I drew nearer, I could feel my heart pounding heavier and heavier. I slowly lowered to my knees.

I was only a few feet from the creature, and I could see it really good. It was a grasshopper, all right, but it looked like some sort of machine. Like it was some kind of mechanical, motorized grasshopper.

Which was impossible, of course—but that's what it looked like.

"Hey there, buddy," I whispered, leaning closer and closer to the insect. *"I'm not going to hurt you. I just need you to hang out for a while so people will believe me."*

I leaned closer still. Sensing my presence, the insect took several small steps backward.

I realized that if I didn't make my move, I risked losing the bug altogether. Catching insects is a lot like catching frogs. If you're not quick, you'll never catch them.

I sprang, snapping the jar out and over the insect. I had to be careful, since the floor of the garage is made of cement, and the jar is glass. If I smacked it down too hard, the glass might crack or break.

But it didn't. And better still—

I caught the grasshopper!

He hopped up and down, up and down, smacking against the glass, and it sounded like a knife tapping a window. The creature must really be made out of some kind of metal!

Very carefully, I lifted the edge of the glass and slid the lid underneath. After a moment of wiggling, I was able to get the lid on. Then I picked it up and screwed it on tight.

And the jar felt heavy! Man! The insect must weigh a pound!

I felt like jumping up and down. I couldn't believe my luck! I had to show Mandy right away.

I hurried out the garage door and out the driveway, stopping only long enough to make sure there were no cars coming. We live in a small subdivision, and not too many cars go by, but you've got to be careful, anyway.

I didn't see any cars . . . but another thing I didn't see was the dark figure hiding in the bushes near Mandy's house—and I didn't even see him until it was too late.

I caught a movement off to the side, just in time to see a water balloon leave the hand of Eddie Finkbinder. Eddie is a pitcher on the school baseball team, and he has a pitching arm that's as fast as a rattlesnake.

I tried to get out of the way of the oncoming projectile, knowing that if I didn't I was in for a good soaker.

And I almost made it.

Almost.

Because the water balloon hit my arm and exploded, spraying me with chilly water.

But that wasn't the worst part.

The jolt had caused me to lose my grip on the jar. Suddenly, it was sent flying into the air, out of my grasp.

Oh no! My jar . . . and my silver grasshopper . . . were going to smash into a million pieces!

5

I heard Eddie laughing as the jar flew up into the air.

"Bullseye!" he shouted.

But I was too worried about breaking the jar and losing my grasshopper to even care what he was saying or doing.

I leapt forward and dove. I knew that my chances of catching the jar in mid-air weren't very good, but I had to try.

I *had* to.

I threw myself forward, arms outstretched like a football player trying to catch a pass. My eyes never left the jar that tumbled through the air. I could still hear Eddie Finkbinder laughing at me, but I didn't pay any attention. I was too focused on the jar.

And at the very last second, I knew I wasn't going to catch it. The jar was just out of reach, just a hair too far to grab onto. I could see the silver grasshopper inside the glass, fluttering around like a mad fishing lure.

I reached, reached, as far as I could—

My fingers touched the jar. I couldn't catch it, but my fingers touching the jar knocked it up into the air just enough to break its fall. The jar hit the grass hard, but it didn't break. My elbows plunged into the grass at the exact same time. It hurt, but I didn't care. I was just glad that the jar hadn't broken.

"Hahaha!" chortled Eddie. "That was a good one, squirrel-breath!" he sneered. Then he lobbed another water balloon.

I was ready this time, and I easily got out of the way of the red blob heading for me.

"I missed on purpose," Eddie claimed.

Oh man, I thought. *I'm in for it now. Eddie is going to squish me like a blueberry.*

But he didn't. Instead, he turned, shook his head, and walked away. "You're no fun," he said. But I think he only left because he ran out of water balloons.

Whatever the reason, I was glad.

But sadly, I had another problem.

My grasshopper wasn't moving. It was just laying at the bottom of the jar on its side. I was certain that the fall had killed it.

Now I was mad. I was mad and I was sad. I didn't want to hurt it, but now it was too late.

I stared at the creature for a few moments, and decided to show Mandy anyway. Even if the grasshopper wasn't alive, she'd still want to see it.

I walked up to her door and knocked, but no one answered. I knocked again and called out her name.

Still no answer.

Darn, I thought. I was hoping that she would have been home.

I turned around and walked back to my house. It was time for dinner, anyway. At least I would be able to show Mom and Dad what I found. I have an older sister named Lisa, but I'm sure she wouldn't care at all. She hates bugs.

When Dad got home, I showed him my grasshopper. He said he thought it looked really cool, but I don't think he believed me when I told him it had been alive. Mom didn't either. I tried to explain, but they just rolled their eyes.

But I knew Mandy would believe me. She had been with me at the river on the day I had first discovered one of the strange silver insects.

I called her on the phone, but no one answered. The answering machine picked up and I left a message for her to call me in the morning.

I took my jar and placed it on my dresser. Even though the grasshopper was dead, it was still pretty cool looking. When school started back up in the fall, I planned on taking it in for show and tell.

Mandy didn't call me back, and I figured that she'd gone to the movies or something with her mom and dad. I watched television for a while, then read a book in bed until I got tired. I could hear the soft murmur of crickets outside my open window, and I heard a car drive by on the street. My eyes grew heavy.

I fell asleep.

When I awoke in the morning, I knew something was wrong.

I could *feel* it. I just had some kind of creepy feeling that all was not well.

And I was right.

I got out of bed.

Suddenly, I gasped.

Then I gasped again.

The mayonnaise jar on my dresser was still there, but there was a large hole in the lid!

The jar was empty!

I spun, expecting to see the silver grasshopper sitting on the floor. I expected to see him on my chair, maybe, or even on a book shelf. I expected that he'd be right around the room somewhere.

What I didn't expect to see was the dollar-sized hole in my screen. It looked like it had been chewed away by something with razor-sharp teeth.

There was a hole in the jar, a hole in the screen . . . *and my silver grasshopper was nowhere to be found!*

And that was just the beginning of how we discovered that the silver metal insects weren't bugs, after all.

What I didn't know at the time was that there were a lot more . . . thousands more.

They were ugly.

They were dangerous.

And they were about to invade.

FUN FACTS ABOUT MINNESOTA:

State Capitol: St. Paul

State Gemstone: Lake Superior agate

State Beverage: Milk

State Bird: Common loon

State Insect: Monarch butterfly

State Tree: Norway pine

State Fish: Walleye

State Flower: Pink and white lady's slipper

State Mushroom: Morel

The total area of Minnesota is 86,943 square miles!

INTERESTING MINNESOTA TRIVIA!

☞ The Mall of America is the size of 78 football fields!

☞ Minnesota has 90,000 miles of shoreline - more than California, Hawaii, and Florida combined!

☞ 'Little House on the Prairie' author Laura Ingalls Wilder lived on Plum Creek, near Walnut Grove.

☞ Tonka trucks were first developed in Minnetonka, Minnesota. They are still made there today!

☞ Minnesota was the 32nd state admitted to the union.

☞ In December of 1889, The Minneapolis Public Library became the first library in the nation to separate children's books from the rest of the collection . . . becoming the first library in the nation to have a 'Children's library'.

ATTENTION YOUNG AUTHORS!
DON'T MISS

JOHNATHAN RAND'S

AUTHOR QUEST ®

THE DEFINITIVE WRITER'S CAMP
FOR SERIOUS YOUNG WRITERS ©

If you want to sharpen your writing skills, become a better writer, and have a blast, Johnathan Rand's Author Quest is for you!

Designed exclusively for young writers, Author Quest is 4 days/3 nights of writing courses, instruction, and classes at Camp Ocqueoc, nestled in the secluded wilds of northern lower Michigan. Oh, there are lots of other fun indoor and outdoor activities, too . . . but the main focus of Author Quest is about becoming an even better writer! Instructors include published authors and (of course!) Johnathan Rand. No matter what kind of writing you enjoy: fiction, non-fiction, fantasy, thriller/horror, humor, mystery, history . . . this camp is designed for writers who have this in common: they LOVE to write, and they want to improve their skills!

For complete details and an application, visit:

www.americanchillers.com

ABOUT THE AUTHOR

ohnathan Rand is the author of more than 65 books, with well
ver 4 million copies in print. Series include **AMERICAN
CHILLERS, MICHIGAN CHILLERS, FREDDIE
FERNORTNER, FEARLESS FIRST GRADER,** and **THE
ADVENTURE CLUB.** He's also co-authored a novel for teens
with Christopher Knight) entitled **PANDEMIA.** When not trav-
ling, Rand lives in northern Michigan with his wife and three
ogs. He is also the only author in the world to have a store that
ells only his works: **CHILLERMANIA!** is located in Indian
iver, Michigan. Johnathan Rand is not always at the store, but he
as been known to drop by frequently. Find out more at:

www.americanchillers.com

Join the official

AMERICAN CHILLERS®

FAN CLUB!

Visit www.americanchillers.com for details

All AudioCraft books are proudly printed, bound, and manufactured in the United States of America, utilizing American resources, labor, and materials.

USA